NILTAVA IN THE OAK TREE

RINU. R

Chennai • Bangalore

CLEVER FOX PUBLISHING
Chennai, India

Published by CLEVER FOX PUBLISHING 2026

ISBN: 978-93-7500-312-0

CONTENTS

1

POISON DAMSEL IN THE WINDOW

They say she poisoned her husband.

I press the office bag to my chest, and silently warn my right leg not to jiggle up and down. I look up at the broody, low-hanging dark clouds. It's time for me to leave for the library, and I hope it doesn't rain on my way there. But I don't move, hoping to catch a glimpse of her before I leave.

They say she poisoned her husband, but I'm not one of them. I don't believe she poisoned her husband, who was ten years her senior. Being neighbours, I had known him my entire life, but I wouldn't call him my friend.

Whispers coated with malice float around her house unfailingly every day, and, most times, I inadvertently stumble upon them.

Becoming a widow within a year of marriage. So sad!

But she never loved him.

She might have plotted to kill him even before their marriage.

Why marry then? Family pressure.

Poor, poor man! Died at 35! Such a waste of a young life!

By the way, I don't mean to say anything ill about the dead, but he looked like an older brother to her than her husband.

I know, right?

I'm not saying they didn't look good together, but—

Don't worry, I know you mean no ill—

But why kill the poor man? The poor, poor young man!

So engrossed are the whisperers and gossipers in their fanciful speculation that they don't see me lurking nearby.

Before my mother comes out of the kitchen and finds me sitting on the porch chair, staring at my neighbor's house, I jump to my feet and gallop out of the house. Rain or no rain, I have to go to work.

......

What happens when one day you wake up, and suddenly you see that someone you love has changed in character? I wonder as I return to my seat after shelving returned books.

My eyes sweep over the sea of myriad faces, their eyes glued to books, newspapers, or journals before them. Like always, I cannot stop wondering what their lives are like. Diverse, yet they all look the same with their lowered heads, connected by the same desire to expand knowledge or traverse a new world on pages.

I unzip my laptop bag, and take out a weighty tome, then plop it on my desk. It's a book spread across three different time periods, not something I usually enjoy reading.

Two pages later, I moan internally. Despite trying hard, I cannot bring myself to be interested in the book. I lift my eyes and allow them to run over the colourful faces in the reading room. What are the dissatisfactions in their lives? What are the dissatisfactions in Eena's life? That's her name. My neighbor's name — Eena. What were her parents thinking, naming her Eena, which translates to mirror in Hindi?

A muffled giggle meets my eardrums, and I immediately look for the culprit. Two young girls with their heads leaning on the table briefly become the focus of attention for others around. Oh, so they're the cause of the disruption. The girls remain in that position, not daring to lift their heads, perhaps fearing the escape of their suppressed mirth.

When the library falls quiet again, I begrudgingly divert my attention back to the tome. I wish I was somewhere else. I wish I was working in another library — the library of my dreams.

The library of my dreams, situated an hour's drive from my house, is a renowned library in the city. Structured in colonial architecture, it has a central hall with a high dome and a series of alcoves housing the different sections of the library. It has a rich collection of books on history, philosophy, literature, science and technology, as well as books on art, music, and culture. It is not only a place to read, but also a hub for various cultural activities and events. The library hosts regular workshops, seminars, and talks by prominent authors and artists from around the world.

I look up from the book to see a bespectacled young man standing by my desk. "I want to return this book," he says, placing a copy of *Oliver Twist* on the desk, seemingly looking pleased with himself for speaking in English. Only a month ago, he asked me if I knew any good English coaching centre, and I offered him the information of the library of my dreams, which also offers English language courses for students and professionals. It seems he joined there.

"Did you like it?" I ask, and watch with amusement a noticeable moment of hesitation slipping across the guy's face. I smile broadly when a hesitant smile unfurls on his face.

"Yes, yes, I did."

I know it is a lie. I didn't like Oliver Twist when I read it. I give a nod, and watch him walk towards an empty seat. But noticing the seats nearby occupied by three girls deters him from sitting there. He spins around and scans the reading room for other empty seats. There were many, but the young man chose the one nestled among bookish boys .

......

I slurp my tea to ward off my mother. It doesn't work. While my mouth hungrily devours the sweet, hot beverage, my eyes eagerly search for Eena to appear at her living room window.

I slurp again, but my mother stays rooted by the front door. I ignore her piercing, disapproving gaze.

"What are you looking at?" she asks, and I fervently hope she doesn't step into the veranda.

I wonder if I should answer her or not. I don't want to encourage her and prolong her stay.

"Nothing," I say, briefly shifting my eyes to a papaya tree.

A moment later, my eyes slip back to where they wants to be.

"How was work?"

I know why she's asking me these generic questions. But I don't relent. The sound of the pressure cooker whistle comes to my rescue, and my mother reluctantly turns and disappears into the house.

Then it begins to rain.

I like the sound of rain beating down. But I'm annoyed because it obstructs my view of her living room window. I check the time on my wristwatch. It's almost time for her to make an appearance at her window. As per my observation, twice a day, she sits by her living room window, gazing either at the street or the mercurial sky. The sky holds her attention more than the street. Perhaps it's because of the gossip mongers traipsing back and forth by her house, looking for something, anything, to tittle-tattle.

Shortly after a rumble from the bleak sky, the rain fury subsides.

My tea is over, and Eena appears in the window. She's watching the drizzle, and I wonder if she knows I'm watching her. I suddenly wish I was a writer, and she, my main character. I could have given her specially curated thoughts to think. I wish I could be privy to her thoughts.

Eena watches the meek raindrops, and I wonder what she sees in them. Rain is enjoyable, but not in excess. Excess can be lethal. Too much rain or heat destroys life. Too much sugar expands the waistline. Too much bitterness and resentment ruin relationships. What happens when there's too much silence between partners? What happens when neither of the partners tries to, or wants to, fill up the burgeoning silence?

The day was depressingly hot when I saw her for the first time. She's pretty, was my first thought. As per my mother's snooping, we weren't the only ones who hadn't received any wedding invitation from our dead neighbour. No one had. And why would anyone, considering he wasn't close to anyone in the neighbourhood. His parents died in a car accident over a decade ago when he was away on a trip with his friends. I was a teen then, and don't remember much about him before his parents' accident. However, after the accident, I began to notice him more, how he avoided interacting with anyone, how he'd keep his head down while walking on the street. I kind of felt pity for him for the influx of relatives in his house prior to his wedding.

She's pretty, was my first thought, and it bothered me. Why would she marry him? I didn't have to wait much, as the notorious busybodies in the neighborhood began circulating tidbits about her around.

It's an arranged marriage, and she's a freelance social media specialist.

When my dead neighbor was alive, I didn't dare watch his wife as unabashedly as I do now. But I did observe them now and then. And it didn't escape my notice how they behaved more like strangers than married couples.

I rarely see her go out.

Is she glad her husband is gone?

Does she feel lonely? Or, does she prefer this to the suffocating silence that existed between her and her late husband?

Will she remarry?

I feel eyes on my back, and I know it before I twist my neck to meet the disapproving gaze of my mother.

She caught me! I clear my throat, gratuitously.

"Aren't you going to change your clothes? Or, are you planning to sit here all night, staring at others' houses?"

There's no motherly warmth in her words. I rise to my feet and without looking at Eena's house, rush to my bedroom.

••••••

I regret bringing the weighty tome with me as I close it. I finally admit to myself that I'm not interested in it, nor can I bring myself to continue reading it.

That's just in our nature, isn't it? Persisting with the belief that if we put enough effort we can make it work. Turn around our failing business. Reverse the rapidly deteriorating health. Work out the struggling relationship. But, sometimes, we just have to let go.

For years, I watched my mother trying to make her marriage work. My father was a perpetually dissatisfied person and a chronic complainer. Before their marriage dissolved, I saw my mother walking on a tightrope all the time. She tried but failed miserably to make her crumbling marriage work. She never divulged to me, but I knew how heartbreaking it must have been to finally confront the futility of her persistence.

My eyes sail over the faces in the reading room. I notice the giggling girls are back, and one is whispering something to the other. I ignore them. Unless they chat out loud, I have nothing to complain about.

The *Oliver Twist* guy is also sitting in a corner, probably with another classic novel he wouldn't enjoy. Two rows from him, two heads also seem to be conversing quietly. One head shakes, and looks ahead briefly, and I catch my breath. It's Eena. It's Eena, I tell myself, twice, then thrice, to convince myself to believe what I'm seeing. She is conversing with a man. And she is smiling. She seems happy. How? Why?

As in with her case, I gawk unabashedly at her, and her companion. Who is he? What is he doing in a public library on a Tuesday morning? Doesn't he work? Can he be a male relative? But, that smile on her face isn't one for a relative. Why doesn't she look in my direction? Why is she smiling so broadly? I feel a fluttering in my chest, and I look away briefly to calm myself. How can she be so happy when her husband just died recently? Doesn't she miss him, or is she glad he's gone? I turn back to her. Oh, she definitely looks glad he's gone. A niggling urge to go there and disrupt their conversation takes over me. I clamp down on that urge by opening the abandoned tome and forcing myself to read. Sure, I am not able to focus. My eyes swim over word after word without absorbing their meaning. I've never seen her look so happy. Why is she looking so happy?

After what feels like eternity, I look up, hungrily. Where is she? Her male companion's attention is now on a book before him. Who the devil is he? My eyes frantically prance all over the reading room. I almost jump out of my seat, but stopped in time. There she is, with a book and a magazine in her hands. She slides back into the seat next to him. What is she reading? Does that book cover look like *One Hundred Years of Solitude?* Why is she reading that? It's one of those books that people talk about with almost religious deference, so I decided to give it a try in my college days. And failed miserably! How can someone enjoy it? But I kept that contentious thought to myself. Never shared it with anyone. Not that anyone cares.

Should I go and tell her that she'll not enjoy that book? But who am I to make such judgement? What if she enjoys it?

What if she finishes reading it? Something I wasn't able to do. The thought bothers me. Not only does she look happy in the company of a man I don't know, after getting rid of her husband, but she somehow manages to finish the book I couldn't.

Somehow, that reminds me of a book I read not long ago, *An Anthropologist on Mars,* by Oliver Sacks, where a painter goes colour-blind after a concussion. Everything appears black and white, or gray to him. Everything, from food, objects to his wife is leached of their colour. He falls into deep sadness and despair.

Aren't colours like happiness? We're drawn to one just like we're drawn to the other. We all seek happiness. So what happens when happiness is sucked out of your life? You search for the cause of its departure and upon finding it, you destroy it, and reclaim your lost happiness.

Is this how she reclaims her happiness? I try to study Eena and the person making her smile. They're quiet, their attention respectively focusing on the reading material before them. I feel that my day is ruined.

......

The tea from the tea kiosk across the library tastes sour in my mouth. I move my head side to side to shake off the image of Eena and her mystery man, sitting side by side, having a cozy chat that I'm not privy to. It's the third day I'm seeing them together. And it's been a week since I saw her in her living room window.

The sour taste doesn't go away. I take two quick huge gulps of the tea, scalding my mouth, and finish it.

I don't want to go back to the library. I don't want to witness them whispering to each other. That's what they do most of the time. Whisper! Making it impossible for me to complain to them for disrupting the peace of the library. But even if they talk aloud, I am not sure I'm brave enough to complain and make myself visible to her. This begs the question — hasn't she noticed me yet? She hasn't looked in my direction, not even once. But if she has, hasn't she recognised me as her neighbour? There's no way she hasn't seen me around my house for a year!

Against my heart's wish, I trod to my workplace.

I avoid looking at the reading room. For five minutes. Then, ten. Then, I cannot take it any longer.

There they are, back to their usual business, mystery man and Eena's face just inches apart, and mystery man saying something to her.

Maybe there is truth in what they say.

Maybe she poisoned her husband.

2

RED FOR A WITCH

Her eyes soaked up the scene before her.

Her uncle, looking like a petulant little boy, sat in a mustard lounge chair. A filigree vase atop a small round side table held a slouchy pink and white striped petunia. Cherry-red wine wall stood in the background; artificial vines with lights graced the wall behind a mango green velvet sofa.

She took a few steps and paused before a big, decorative mirror. She recalled her mother whispering in her ear, many moons ago, on one of their visits to the house that the mirror had magical powers just like the magic mirror in the story *Snow* White. Unlike the evil queen, Prisha didn't bother asking the mirror who was the fairest of them all, but instead opened her mouth and bared her teeth. She flinched.

"Awful!"

Prisha looked at her uncle. The petulant look was replaced by disapproval.

"Don't you brush your teeth regularly? You eat sweets a lot, don't you?" He paused, gave a dramatic sigh and continued, "Your mother is to blame. She spoiled you!"

Abashed, Prisha hung her head. She wiggled her toes and frowned at her chipped lemon green nail polish that her mother had applied the previous night.

"Is someone talking about me?" Prisha's mother entered the living room, the end of her pink and white floral saree's pallu nearly brushing the white marble floor.

Prisha's eyes alternated between her uncle and her mother. Her uncle snapped his head to the side, pouting.

"We did what we could, Daiwik. If she doesn't like you, we cannot do anything," her mother said, attempting to placate her uncle's sour mood.

Prisha watched her uncle intently. His expression didn't change.

"All we could do was take the marriage proposal to her. What can we do if she has no feelings for you?"

"Her parents approve of me," he said.

"Well, you're not marrying her parents!" her mother retorted, slightly miffed.

Her uncle didn't respond.

The indefatigable cacophony of the crows conferencing at the terrace wall of the neighbor, lured Prisha's rickety grandmother out of her room. With wobbly feet, she crossed the hallway and stood by one of the many large windows of the living room.

Prisha's grandmother peered at the black birds. "Something is wrong," she said.

"One of their own must have died," reasoned her mother.

"Harbinger of doom," Prisha's uncle voiced his opinion about the black birds.

"Oh, come on," her mother uttered, disbelievingly.

Prisha's grandmother turned her rheumy eyes to her daughter, and said, "They follow you, don't they?"

"Are you serious, Maa?" Prisha's mother questioned. A playful smile danced on her lips.

Prisha wanted to ask what they were talking about but she remained mum. Her questions were rarely answered, and she had no intention of disappointing herself by asking questions that would remain unanswered.

"Look at him," Prisha's mother smirked and gestured to her younger brother. "He's sulking because of the rejection."

Prisha's grandmother frowned. "What nonsense! As far as I know she isn't the last woman on Earth."

"But I like her," her uncle grumbled.

"Well, it's of no use!"

"But—

"There's no 'but' after someone explicitly expresses their lack of interest in you. Just get over it!"

With that, Prisha's grandmother retreated back to her room. Prisha's mother's smirk transmogrified into an eerie smug grin.

Prisha's uncle directed his gaze at her, inducing her mother to do the same.

"Don't you care for your daughter? Look at her teeth! Prisha, open your mouth and show your mother your teeth," her uncle said with the intention of hurting her mother.

He succeeded in his mission. Affronted, her mother opened her mouth, perhaps to retort, but instead clamped her jaw shut. She turned to Prisha, and steered her towards their room.

......

She hadn't seen her father in three months. Although he would call her weekly, he didn't sound like the person she used to know. She had hoped to return home after the end of the summer vacation, but to her surprise and dismay, she was enrolled in a new school in her grandmother's town. Prisha wasn't a fool, but there was nothing wrong with hoping. Neither of her parents said anything explicitly, and they always sidestepped her questions. But she had heard words like 'separate' and 'incompatible' often enough to know something wasn't right with her parents' marriage. Her mother never talked with her father whenever he called. She'd immediately hand over the phone to Prisha.

Prisha wasn't sure how she felt. She didn't dislike living in her grandmother's house, but sometimes she missed her father, and wished they could go back to living the way they were. Something within her told her that it would never happen again. And that saddened her.

Despite the changes in their lives, Prisha's mother remained the way she had always been. She was as effervescent as a butterfly. Her mother walked with a bounce, and carried a smile with her all the time. Her love for shopping showed no signs of abating. She always looked forward to Sunday to take Prisha out shopping. Prisha should have been happier with all the treats, gifts and clothes falling into her lap, but she wasn't. Unlike her mother, they had lost their charm for her. She has had enough.

But she indulged in them, especially chocolates and sweets. She was guilty of that. It was impossible for her not to when they were within her reach. In her room. In the kitchen.

And that had repercussions.

Prisha wasn't a bad looking girl but her teeth were a different story. She rarely smiled or laughed baring her teeth.

"Like a smiley face emoji." Her mother had joked once seeing Prisha's closed-mouth smile too many times. But Prisha was hurt and felt indignant. She believed it was her mother's responsibility to care for her, and her teeth. Of course, her mother couldn't be ignorant of how bad her teeth were!

"It's yellow. Like light, dirty yellow," one of her classmates, Yana, had said, one unusually warm mid November morning. Her friend, to whom Yana was explaining the color of a dress her elder sister had received on her birthday, looked confused. Yana's eyes lit up upon seeing Prisha, and she pointed at her and shouted, "Like Prisha's teeth!"

"Beta, don't eat too much chocolate. It's not good for your teeth." Her father had cautioned her one night, when he found her stuffing chocolates into her mouth after dinner.

Her mother suddenly materialized as if out of thin air. Her aggressive stance told Prisha that an ugly argument was about to ensue.

"Why can't she eat them? I brought those chocolates for her," Her mother said with an edge in her voice.

"Because that's what she eats all the time. Sweets and chocolates! It's not good for her teeth. Have you seen her teeth?"

"Oh, so, now you think I don't care about my own daughter?" Her mother had fumed.

......

Standing on the lawn in her grandmother's sprawling garden, Prisha watched a couple of doves.

Strutting and with a puffed chest, a dove with iridescent green and purple feathers around its neck approached another with less iridescence. Prisha knew enough about birds to know that the strutting one was the male and the other, female. When the flamboyant male neared the female, she flew away, and the male looked on, stunned.

Prisha laughed aloud and heard someone clear his throat.

Prisha suddenly realized she wasn't alone in the garden. She turned sideways and found their middle-aged gardener cutting a few branches of a medium sized tree.

"What are you doing?" She asked, moving closer to the tree.

"When left to their own devices, they grow wild and unruly," the gardener said.

Prisha didn't think there was anything wrong with that.

"So you're taking away their freedom to grow the way they want?"

The gardener paused, and looked at her. Though his face was impassive, discomfort descended on Prisha. He turned back to his work.

"No, actually pruning encourages regrowth. I'm just removing broken and damaged branches," the gardener said.

"Really?"

With his back to her, he said, "If there is something in your life that keeps you from growing unhindered, then you should remove it from your life."

Prisha didn't say anything.

"Oh, you're here! Prisha, I was looking for you all over the house. I have made onion pakoras for you. Come inside and eat." Her mother suddenly appeared from behind them.

Prisha didn't move.

"It's beautiful," her mother said breezily, as her eyes glided over the well-maintained garden.

Prisha cast a furtive glance at the gardener. Her mother's commendation had swelled his chest. It suddenly reminded her of the male dove.

"Prisha, let's go inside," her mother said, turning to her.

"Just five more minutes," Prisha entreated.

Her mother sighed dramatically. "Fine. Five more minutes, and then you need to come inside."

Her mother walked back to the house.

Prisha looked around herself. Her own chest swelled in pride when she realized she knew the names of some of the flowers before her: Chrysanthemum, Marigold, Rose, Carnation, Petunia, Spider Lily. Though distinct in their appearance, one thing was common in them: they were all red in color.

Maybe the gardener was watching her, and maybe, he had the power to read minds, for he said, "Your mother's favorite color."

Suddenly, it sparked a memory from her childhood. Her mother standing before a mirror, wearing a plain blood red saree, tips of her hair lifting all around her, like static strands.

……

She waited for the call, but it never came. It was the first time since she and her mother came to live with her grandmother that a whole week had rolled by without receiving a call from her father.

She tried her best not to spill out her emotions, but it was hard not to be irked by her mother's smug expression. She prepared her ears to hear her mother's insight on her 'uncaring' father any moment.

Your father didn't call you, did he? Well, don't be disappointed. That's what happens when you put too much trust on someone. He's probably busy like he always has been. He has no time for family.

Prisha alighted from her school bus and turned into her street. She frowned at her unpolished shoes and recalled for the fifth time the scolding she had received because of it. Not only had she forgotten about it because her mind was preoccupied with worrying about the math test that morning, but it had skipped her mother's notice too. It had never happened before.

Around fifty meters from her grandmother's house, Prisha stopped. She didn't want to go home. She didn't want to see her mother. She was mad at her mother and believed that seeing her might threaten her attempt to clamp down on her suppressed emotions. So she backtracked. She hadn't covered even six meters before she heard a familiar voice calling her name.

She got caught. Her heart wasn't happy about it and thudded against her chest. Prisha turned to see her grandmother's gardener walking towards her.

"Where are you going?" he asked.

Prisha didn't respond nor did she meet his eyes.

"Go home."

Prisha nodded and bolted to her grandmother's house.

When she entered the house gate, she was graced with the sight of her mother, grandmother and uncle lounging in the garden seating area. Three pairs of eyes turned to her, augmenting her discomfort. Reluctantly, she turned to them.

"How was the math test, Prisha?" Her mother asked, with a smile that didn't reach her eyes.

Her suppressed emotions began to unspool, and her voice held an edge as she said, "I got scolded for wearing unpolished shoes."

"Were they unpolished?" Her mother said, rhetorically. Prisha didn't say anything and looked away. Her eyes landed on a white sculpture of a scantily clad woman holding a water pot at the foot of the fish pond. The disappointment of learning that the pond had no fish in it, on the first day of her arrival, washed over her once again. A laugh snapped her out of her despondency. She turned to her uncle, his laugh now tapering to a smirk as he looked back and forth between his sister and niece.

"Your mother used to get scolded twice a week for wearing dirty shoes," her uncle recounted.

Her grandmother closed her eyes and shook her head. "She'd do it deliberately," she said.

"What do you mean?" Prisha asked curiously.

Her grandmother opened her rheumy eyes, and transfixed her with a penetrating gaze. "I would send your mother in a clean and ironed school uniform, and polished shoes, but somehow she'd manage to dirty her shoes, and sometimes her uniform before reaching school."

Surprised, Prisha turned to her mother. "Why?"

"Why? Because your mother hates to play by the rules," her uncle answered for her mother.

Prisha's mother rubbed the side of her eyes. "My head is aching," she muttered.

"Go and lie down for a while," advised Prisha's grandmother.

Prisha's mother rose from the garden chair. "Come, Prisha," she said without looking at Prisha.

"Let her be with me for a minute," Prisha's grandmother said, and Prisha watched her mother vanish into the house.

Her uncle rose to his feet, his eyes glued to his phone. "I'm going out. Need to meet someone," he said to no one in particular.

"Who?" Prisha's grandmother asked, drawing a slight scowl on her son's face.

"I'm not a child, Ma, to tell you everything." With that, he walked away.

"Well, he behaves like a child most of the time," Prisha's grandmother grumbled with a disapproving gaze at the receding figure of her son.

Prisha occupied the seat left by her mother.

Her grandmother shifted her gaze to her. "Are you upset or angry?"

Prisha mulled over the question briefly. She was upset that her father didn't call her. She was mad at her mother for not polishing her shoes, and bringing the ire of her teacher on her. She was upset that her parents were not on speaking terms, and angry at herself for not resisting herself from eating sweets and chocolates, thus damaging her teeth further.

"I'm not sure." A safe answer that didn't require further explanation, Prisha thought, as she voiced it out loud.

"We're always sure, but believe we aren't. If something is upsetting you, you already know what it is," her grandmother said. Her eyes then glided down and paused on the three empty ceramic coffee mugs on the center table, "Can you guess which one is your mother's?"

Prisha's eyes followed her grandmother's. It wasn't hard. One was lemon green, another white with blue and green floral designs, and the third one, red.

"The red one."

Her grandmother closed her eyes and nodded. When she opened them, she looked at her grandchild, and leaned her head as if sharing a secret with her, "Since you've known your mother for thirteen years, you probably know that she's a very stubborn woman. There's no way you can dissuade her from doing what she wants to do. Anger can do no one any good, but your mother uses it as a weapon to get whatever she wants. She also has difficulty in curbing her emotions. Don't be like her. I'm not saying you repress your pent-up emotions but when it's about anger, don't hoard it and unleash it as a weapon. Instead, release it into the wind.

......

The wind inadvertently carried secret whispers, gossip, and half-baked truths.

During lunch break, Prisha learned that the mother of one of her classmates, Krutika, one of the smartest kids in her class, was not her biological mother, but step mother.

It uncorked a memory. When she was eight years old, in one of her visits to her paternal grandparents house, she witnessed a squabble between her mother and a maid. Later in the day, Prisha, accidentally overheard the rankled maid telling another maid of the neighbor that Prisha's mother was a witch.

A witch.

Not only was her mother a witch, according to the rankled maid, but Prisha was conceived out of her sorcery. Prisha's mother had failed to conceive for many years, then one day, she announced she was pregnant. It happened on the same day that a neighbor lost their child in an accident. What a coincidence, the neighbors murmured.

Prisha's droopy eyes held the History notebook, lying on the study table before her, with loathing. She hated the subject along with maths. She rose from her seat and headed to her bed. It happened all the time. Whenever she'd sit to study history or math, her bed would beckon her.

She lay on her bed and closed her eyes.

"Why are you sleeping now?"

Groaning, Prisha hauled herself into a sitting position. Her mother entered the room and stood by her study table.

"Is boring history making you sleepy, Prisha? If this continues, you'll get bad grades in your next test as well," her mother said.

Prisha pursed her lips. "I don't understand why we need to learn and memorize the events and dates of the past. Not like the recent past, but the long past! Not important. Also there are tons of names of long dead humans. How am I going to benefit from remembering what war they fought and how they died? I don't care!"

Her mother smiled. "I understand," she said, and her eyes roved over the room, and returned to her daughter. "I noticed you were in a sour mood when you returned from school. What happened? Did you get scolded by any teacher? It couldn't be your shoes as I polished them nicely today."

"No, not the shoes," Prisha mumbled.

"It's your father, isn't it? Because he didn't call you?"

Prisha didn't say anything. She turned her gaze down to the floral bed sheet.

"Alright, if you're sleepy, then sleep, but be up before dinner," her mother said, and left her room.

Two hours later, Prisha sat at the dinner table, listening to the adults talk with disinterest. After twenty minutes, she got up from her seat, having finished her meal. She went to the living room to watch TV, and soon afterward, her mother joined her on the sofa.

Halfway into a TV show, Prisha's mother's phone began ringing. With one look at her screen, and a smile crinkling her eyes, Prisha's mother handed the phone to her.

Prisha's face lit up, and she answered the call immediately, "Hi, dad."

3

NILTAVA IN THE OAK TREE

"An apple a day keeps the doctor away," said Mouni, biting into the crunchy apple from her friend's orchard.

Pratibha sighed. "If only that were the case. My husband used to have apples almost every day, but cancer ultimately took him away."

Mouni looked away. She knew that was coming. Pratibha never missed a chance to weave details of her late husband into every conversation. Mouni couldn't understand why Pratibha constantly resurrected the memory of her dead spouse, particularly since she had never loved him. Pratibha, in fact, despised him. Mouni could nearly picture the relief Pratibha must have felt when her husband took his last breath. Those unfamiliar with Pratibha saw her as a perpetually grieving wife. What a shame!

Pratibha rose from her seat and winced. "My knees hurt when I am on my feet. I wish something would magically transport me home. Oh, I nearly forgot! I need to get some groceries. If you need anything, you can join me."

Mouni shook her head. "Not today. Thanks for the apple."

Pratibha gave a wave and was gone.

Mouni threw the apple core into her garden. A gentle rustle of leaves to her left drew her gaze in that direction. Mouni held her breath, then slowly released it when no other sound followed. Clusters of tall trees with clinging creepers and hanging climbers mutely stared at her. Her eyes roved beyond the garden and into the woods.

Mouni wasn't paranoid and was confident she wouldn't end up like other elderly people. She was determined not to lose her mind. She didn't believe in spirits or ghosts either. That's why it bothered her. It wasn't her imagination.

She had heard the sound of leaves stirring when there was no breeze, and the crunching of parched leaves. Intruders? That's one of the drawbacks of living near nature; danger could be lurking around and you wouldn't even know.

Twice she had thought of telling Pratibha about it but decided against it at the last moment. She knew what Pratibha's response would be.

It's your husband's spirit.

Mouni stared at the towering oak tree as she rose from her seat on the patio and walked inside.

......

Mouni glanced at the wall clock for the third time before heading to the porch. The sky was clear and the air pleasantly warm. It was the tourist season. A time of the year when tourist influx choked Himachal roads.

Her eyes surveyed the path to her home. It was empty.

Pratibha should have arrived by then. What was taking her so long? Could she have canceled her plans to come? Mouni wondered. It would be unusual if she didn't turn up. Since her husband's death two months ago, it had become a regular practice for Pratibha to stop by and see Mouni every morning. Two widows talking about nothing in particular over a cup of mid morning tea.

They had been friends for almost two decades. But they weren't the kind of friends who would confide in each other without worrying about the others' reaction. In fact, it wasn't their mutual likeness that made them friends, but their late husband's friendship.

When Mouni's husband, an IAS officer, was posted in Shimla twenty years ago, Mouni was ecstatic. After living in chaotic Delhi her whole life, Mouni was more than ready to move to the hill station. A year after they had moved, they crossed paths with Pratibha and her husband, who were the proprietors of several fruit orchards. The thought of having a personal apple farm fascinated Mouni's husband. With the assistance of Pratibha's husband, Mouni and her husband managed to own an apple farm in Fagu, a serene Himalayan hamlet, within a few years.

After taking voluntary retirement, Mouni and her husband made Shimla their permanent home.

Over the years, Mouni and Pratibha's husband's friendship grew stronger. They visited each other's houses occasionally, and went on trips together. Unlike their spouses, Mouni and Pratibha tolerated each other's presence out of courtesy. They didn't hate nor liked each other. But Mouni disliked Pratibha's daughter wholeheartedly. Pratibha had a son and a daughter. Her daughter, Janvi, was married with two children. Janvi's curiosity or rather perplexity at Mouni's childlessness rankled Mouni, and led to some arguments with her husband.

"I can't see why that'd make you angry. She's just curious," he had said, one evening, after returning from Pratibha's house.

"Curious? What is there to be curious about? This is not the first time she brought up the subject. Can't she see how annoying it is?" Mouni's anger shifted from Janvi to her husband.

Mouni's husband mumbled something incomprehensible. Mouni's heart told her to leave it be. But her mouth didn't oblige.

"What did you say?" She asked.

Mouni's husband took off his wristwatch and placed it on the dresser. He then sat on the bed and removed his socks, "Well, she has two children...."

"So?"

"So, she just doesn't understand why you don't have any. She didn't criticize you or anything. Just curious."

"My life is not her business! Her mother knows that I had a miscarriage."

Mouni's husband gave a mirthless laugh. Mouni clenched her teeth.

"Yeah, right. How can I forget that? That's why we don't have any children. The reason is not because you didn't want any."

"It's not my fault that I had a miscarriage." Mouni was mildly shaking with anger.

Mouni's husband rose from the bed, gave her a look, and walked to the bathroom.

Yes, Mouni didn't want a child and her husband did. Surprisingly, she was unaware of it herself till she got married. When looking at other children didn't ignite the right emotions in her, Mouni realized what she didn't want. The lack of maternal instinct bothered her.

Mouni found herself smiling with relief when she saw Pratibha trudging along the cobbled path. She walked to the patio. Pratibha placed a cloth bag on the foldable table. Mouni didn't bother to look inside it.

"Peaches," said Pratibha, as she sat on the chair facing Mouni. Mouni had guessed so.

"You should stop bringing all these fruits. They'll end up rotting," said Mouni.

Pratibha didn't seem to care. Her eyes lazily watched the deodar trees around. "Make something out of them. Jam, apple pie. Janvi makes desserts from them. Just yesterday she made jam for us, and took some for her family."

Mouni shifted in her seat. She wasn't interested in hearing about Pratibha's nosy daughter. "Why did you get late today?"

Pratibha turned to Mouni with surprise. They weren't close friends. Never bothered to pretend as such. So it was surprising when Mouni expressed her interest in Pratibha's company.

"I wasn't feeling well upon waking. Slept an extra hour."

"Just don't die."

Pratibha regarded her thoughtfully. "Oh, I forgot to tell you. Janvi is pregnant."

Mouni mustered a weak congratulation, and looked sideways at her flower garden. Spring was a riot of colour with daffodils, hydrangeas, magnolias, ornamental cherries, gladiolus and honeysuckle crowding the landscape. Their beauty calmed her instantly. Then, something moved in her peripheral vision and Mouni gasped.

"What happened?" Pratibha queried, as she followed Mouni's gaze to the large oak tree, its gnarled branches stretching both outward and upward into the sky. The tree's bark was festooned with mosses and lichens. A brightly-coloured rufous-bellied Niltava watched them quietly from a low branch. The echoing call of the Indian cuckoo much further away shifted their attention in that direction, and then, at each other.

"What happened?" Pratibha asked again with a frown.

"Nothing. I think I need to get my eyes checked," Mouni said. Oscillopsia. A vision problem in which objects appear to jump and jiggle when they're actually still. That's what she read when she searched the symptoms online the night before.

"Why? Have trouble seeing? It's old age, you know."

Mouni didn't say anything. She looked at the oak tree again. The Niltava was gone.

"Daman would sit here, sometimes for hours, simply watching the myriad of birds coming to the garden. I don't know why, but he suddenly took interest in birds two years ago," said Mouni.

Pratibha looked at Mouni intently. Ironic as it was, Mouni, who had a good relationship with her husband, rarely talked about him, while Pratibha, who had a rocky relationship with her late husband, brought him up in every conversation.

"I have to go to the orchard today. Workers are coming to pick the apples," Pratibha said.

Pratibha had two thousand apple trees in her orchard and hired at least forty migrant workers every harvesting season.

Mouni sold her apple orchard seven months after her husband's funeral. She hated having to hire laborers for handling different aspects of crop management — right from spraying, plucking, packing, loading and fetching the produce for transportation from orchards to the road head.

The high, piercing metallic whistles reached their ears and they turned to the source of the sound. The Niltava was back on the Oak tree, regarding them. It was in the same spot as when they first saw it. A chill ran through Mouni.

"That bird wasn't there a moment ago," she said aloud to herself.

"Huh? No, it was. It was there the whole time," said Pratibha.

Despite its diminutive size, something about its unwavering gaze made Mouni uneasy.

"Why don't you have dinner with me tonight?" Mouni asked, her eyes not leaving the bird.

"Huh?"

"Have dinner with me tonight. I'll make something special." Mouni's voice betrayed her and she sounded almost as though she was pleading. Pratibha's expression flitted between surprise and confusion.

Mouni looked at the cloth bag and said, "You keep bringing all these fruits so I thought…."

Both of them knew that wasn't the reason behind Mouni's dinner offer. Mouni's spontaneous offer surprised even herself.

"I don't know. Maybe some other day. The apple picking—

"Oh, right, I forgot about that. No problem. Some other day."

"Is everything okay, Mouni?" Pratibha couldn't help asking.

"Why?" Mouni concealed her apprehension with a convincing smile.

"Nothing. I should get going now," Pratibha rose from her seat. With a quivering smile, Mouni nodded and watched her leave.

The sudden silence in the air made her look, once again, at the Oak tree. The Niltava was gone.

......

The house they chose was tucked away in the quiet pocket of Chotta Shimla. It was a colonial-era wooden house that boasted floor-to-ceiling glass windows. While Mouni was apprehensive over the wilderness of the area, once there, the stark beauty that engulfed her dispelled her earlier trepidation.

Late December that year, she experienced snow for the first time. One cold January morning, they had a power outage and were without water at home, because some of the pipes had frozen and burst due to the cold. Their mobile batteries were dead. Another first time experience was lighting a candle. The night looked exceptionally beautiful. She and her husband pulled chairs to the front door and watched the snowfall. Some days, at dawn, she'd gaze out of the bedroom window and all she would see was pine, cedar and deodar trees shrouded in mist and blue skies beyond.

Cocooned in the snug swing in the living room, Mouni would read books to her heart's content while her husband tended to the garden.

The first few days of winter were always enjoyable, and the first two or three days of snowfall too. Then, all she could think about was the winter ending.

Mouni scooped a spoonful of warm soup, and blew it a few times before bringing it into her mouth. She had been eating vegetable soup a lot lately. She had been dreaming about her husband a lot lately too. And her husband preferred soup for dinner. Mouni watched the news for a few minutes and changed it to an English comedy show. Twenty minutes later, she turned off the TV and padded to the kitchen.

Carrying a plate of chopped apples and peaches, she walked to the patio. She didn't have the stomach to eat them, but didn't have the heart to see them rot.

The garden was dazed with moonlight. It was still, and the stillness bothered her. She took a piece of apple and bit on it half-heartedly. She wished the wind to blow. She cleared her throat and laughed nervously to create some noise in the still atmosphere. She tried her best to stave off the uneasy feeling creeping in her. Mouni was about to pick a slice of peach, but suddenly froze. She could feel her heart pounding against her rib cage as her eyes struggled to make sense of what she was seeing. Something gleamed from behind the oak tree.

A glint of a knife. Her alarmed mind voiced. No, no, it wasn't! She assured herself.

Sure, it was just the trick of her eyes. When she blinked again, whatever she had believed to have seen was gone. But her petrified heart wouldn't be calmed. A part of her wanted to rush inside and bolt the door, but another part didn't want to give in to the paranoia of old age.

Suddenly, she missed her husband and her eyes welled up. How was she going to live like this? She blinked several times to stop the tears from falling. Mouni picked a slice of peach and bit on it hard. Since she had lost interest in it, she had to chew it several times more than usual to push it down her throat.

Mouni was miffed at Pratibha for not accepting her dinner invitation. She was more annoyed at herself for behaving in a way she hadn't ever before. She never imagined she'd experience things that didn't exist. The nagging feeling that something sinister was lurking in the periphery, watching her, waiting, always waiting, for the right time to harm her.

A week ago, while returning from the market, she felt as if someone was following her. Her rational mind rebuffed her fear, but Mouni couldn't help looking over her shoulder, again and again, till she reached her house. She spent the whole day feeling irritated by the way she handled her fear. Some days, she would hold her breath, trying to pick up on any peculiar sounds nearby. On other days, she'd feel an unsettling sensation of someone being behind her, leading her to leap from her chair, only to find herself alone.

Occasionally, a local Himachali guy — a worker in Pratibha's Apple orchard — used to deliver her groceries to her. But her delusions put a stop to it. She began to suspect him. What if he was the one trying to sneak into her house at night? Not that she'd have any proof or anything. Not that she had seen any intruder near her property. But, then, how to explain the noises she was hearing at the dead of the night? Something was evoking her intrinsic fear. She had been toying with the idea of taking a trip somewhere. Just to get out of the house. But, at the same time, she hated the thought of leaving the house alone. As if the house was a living entity. Maybe it was the old age. She believed she was part of the house, and she couldn't imagine separating from it.

There were times when she was going to tell Pratibha about the voices. Voices of the long dead. But never her husband's voice. Some days, her money would go missing. Someone stole? How? Secretly broke into the house at night and stole the money? Could have harmed her as well! Her anxious mind would chatter on till she was sick.

Mouni didn't want any pity, another reason for her to not disclose her concerns to Pratibha. Pratibha would never voice it, but she would hold Mouni's choice to be child-free as a factor in her present situation. Mouni would never regret her decision to not have kids. Even if she had a child, there was no guarantee her child would have stayed with her.

The sound of the Niltava shook the silent night. Her heart leapt, and Mouni turned to the Oak tree. The darkness around the tree made it impossible to see anything on it. But Mouni was sure that she was hearing things, hallucinating, and no Niltava was on the tree.

Weariness overtook her. Still, she managed to rise from her chair to go inside the house. Leaving the plate on the table, Mouni tightened her shawl around her and moved towards her house. Just then something moved past the living room window. Her heart lurched, and she stopped. She saw something, didn't she? She was certain that she did. Mouni felt dizzy and faltered. She shut her eyes as her head drooped.

To her amazement and utter relief, she heard a familiar voice. First distant, then closer.

"Mouni, what happened? Mouni?"

Mouni turned to her friend. Pratibha visibly struggled to walk as fast as she could, and upon coming closer, examined Mouni with concerned eyes. She touched Mouni's arms while waiting for Mouni to respond.

"Mouni, what is it? Are you not feeling well? Should I call my family doctor? I… I realised something wasn't right when you invited me for dinner. What is it?" Pratibha said.

Mouni wanted to blurt out everything. She glanced at the oak tree and then at her house. The house was empty without her. No shadow or intruder met her eyes. It was safe. As always.

"Mouni?"

Mouni turned to Pratibha and shook her head.

"Let's go inside," said Pratibha and both turned to the house.

4

LIKE A WILD MUSHROOM

The fat gray spider raised its front legs as the broom came closer. They glared at each other. The spider and Juana. Just a swing of the broom would do the deed, but Juana hesitated. It was something about its defensive stance—its front legs still up in the air. Grunting with self-loathing, Juana changed her mind about smacking the thing dead, and instead removed the web, swiftly carrying the spider with it. She sprinted out of the door and towards the gate. But the spider had dropped somewhere on the way. Juana knew it was just a matter of time before the spider found its way back to the house of terror.

"Hey, what are you doing there? I thought you were getting rid of the spiders." Juana turned to her pregnant youngest sister, Javi, standing by the front door.

"I'm," said Juana. Javi was terrified of spiders and couldn't stand them. So Juana, being the big protective sister, had offered to kill them. Then what brought the change of heart? Juana wasn't sure herself. It wasn't in her nature to spare the life of scary-looking insects. But she wasn't going to tell that to her sister.

"Oh, look, they are here," Javi announced excitedly, and began waving at the guests arriving at the gate.

The guests included Juana's other four younger sisters and their families. Just behind them were Javi and her husband's friends. Lucia, Juana's third younger sister, striding ahead of them, stopped three feet from Juana. "Why on Earth are you holding a broom?" She asked.

Juana looked down at her hand. She had forgotten about the broom. She laughed, and her sister joined her.

"She was getting rid of the spiders for me," Javi answered, coming from behind.

Lucia was now joined by Juana's other two sisters, Kaia and Amari, who were also sporting a baby bump. And both were holding the hands of two children each.

Kaia grimaced. "Oh, those ghastly things! They make me shudder. In my home, Tahir deals with them."

With more guests streaming in, they all went inside the house.

Soon, Javi's baby shower started.

......

Juana wasn't proud of what she was about to do. She slammed her palm hard on the car horn. It was futile. Other than drawing in the glares of some frustrated people from the seats of their vehicles, the traffic hadn't moved an inch. Juana dragged her hand over her close-cropped hair to tame a few unruly hairs slouching over her forehead.

Juana hated wasting time. She believed in spending every minute wisely and productively.

Growing up, people around her believed she was very strict with herself. Unlike other parents, Juana's parents didn't harbour high expectations for their children. But that didn't stop her from aiming high.

If Juana hadn't achieved a self-imposed academic goal by a certain date, then she'd cut off her hair. The first time she did it, her mother was appalled and inconsolable. Her mother was in love with her long tresses and nurtured them as if they were her own. But that didn't put an end to Juana's self-castigation. A time came when Juana couldn't see a point in growing her hair long, distressing her mother further.

When she entered academia, everyone extolled her hard work and credited her self-discipline. However, those plaudits soon morphed into grievances when Juana kept warding off prospective proposals of marriage.

Juana's parents' lamentations about her spinsterhood died only after their fourth daughter sprouted her first child. Juana took comfort in the fact that they departed the world having experienced the love of grandchildren galore.

It was the monsoon month of August, and yet the morning was very muggy. Juana cranked up the AC, and leaning back in her seat, she heaved a sigh of relief at the rush of cool air.

Her stomach grumbled from having left home without eating anything. She blamed it on the previous day's event. She had eaten a lot, and on her sisters' insistence, and to avoid inviting any discourse about being an anomalous one in the family, Juana stayed back in Javi's house until very late into the night.

Juana straightened in her seat. The traffic had begun to crawl.

The face of a little girl appeared in the back glass of the car in front of her. They were everywhere. Little humans. Everyone seemed to have one, or two, or more with them. When Juana was in her early thirties, Lucia, then twenty-three and unmarried, shared her eagerness to experience motherhood. Juana was perturbed. Everyone around her was either talking about marriage or children. And she wasn't even thinking about those subjects. For the first time, in the wee dark hours of the night, propped up by mounds of pillows, Juana questioned herself—why wasn't she interested in either marriage or babies? She felt absolutely nothing about those things. What was wrong with her? Of course, she didn't get any answer from herself.

She flipped her wrist to check the time on her wristwatch. She was already late for her first class, and she hated that. She adhered to the virtue of punctuality throughout her life, and breaking that principle, even once, felt sacrilegious.

It took half an hour more before Juana could maneuver her car out of the slow-moving traffic.

••••••

Maya's face lit up, and she enthusiastically pointed ahead. A professor of chemistry and Juana's colleague, Maya was a mycophile. Once every week, during the months of monsoon, both women hiked to regions abundant in wild mushrooms.

Thus far, thanks to Maya, Juana was acquainted with seven mushroom species growing on termite mounds, logs of dead or decaying trees, or rotting plants.

"You have very sharp eyes for your age," remarked Juana as they trudged to a higher plain.

"I'm not that old," said Maya, looking over her shoulder at Juana.

"Yeah, right, being in your late forties is not old at all," said Juana.

"Actually—

Maya didn't say whatever she was about to. Instead, a jarring shriek escaped from her. Maya spun around, coming to stand beside Juana, and clasped her right elbow like a scared child.

Juana followed her eyes and noticed a scruffy man of middle age in tattered clothes lying on the forest floor a few feet to their left. His weather-beaten, craggy face and skin, and ragged walnut T-shirt with dull sage green cotton pants blended well with the surroundings.

Maya's shriek hadn't disturbed him. Juana had seen enough of such men to recognise he was drunk and too impaired for the real world and was probably in a fairyland. It had come to her notice recently that two of her male students consumed alcohol, and, unsurprisingly, both came from troubled families. Worried she might come across as judgmental and her advice as a reprimand, she asked a male colleague to talk to the boys.

"They take alcohol to dull the soreness of their existence," the male colleague had opined, as if vindicating their action, and at the same time dismissing the matter.

"Just a homeless drunk. Let's go," said Juana, and Maya let go of her hand.

They then proceeded to the spot Maya had pointed to. Maya's excitement deflated a bit when she found they were looking at shiitake mushrooms springing from decaying wood. The eight light brown caps with whitish gills, a white spore print, and a light brown stalk with a fuzzy texture failed to satiate Maya's irrepressible appetite for unseen mushroom species. The last two hikes in different parts of the forest had given them the same result.

"They are just shiitake," Maya sounded disappointed. "Why only shiitake?"

"Not going to take them?" Juana asked.

"You know I'm." Maya stooped down but straightened immediately. "You know what? On second thought, I think you should take them. Don't you like mushrooms?" Maya asked.

Juana hesitated a bit before answering, "I'm not exactly a fan of mushrooms. I mean, I have eaten them a few times. I don't dislike them."

Maya smiled. "They are good for you. They are packed with nutrients. Honestly, I have had enough of shiitake mushrooms. So is my family. My children will go crazy if I prepare shiitake tonight. I already made mushrooms twice this week, so I'd rather you take them."

"Or, we can just leave them be. Undisturbed," suggested Juana, and received an appalled look from Maya.

"Seeing a wild edible mushroom and not taking it is almost like desecrating a corpse," Maya said, looking serious.

"Oh, come on!"

While Maya got busy plucking the mushroom, Juana turned to look at the drunk, still lying motionless on the forest floor like a dead log of wood. Juana imagined mushrooms sprouting from his atrophied body one day and was surprised by such an image.

"Aren't they fascinating?" Maya asked, examining a mushroom in her hand, entranced, like she had done countless times before.

Maya wasn't the only one in Juana's proximity drawn to edible fungi. One of Juana's brothers-in-law, a biology researcher, couldn't help bringing up fungi during get-together dinner conversations.

"Such an oddity. They don't try to fit into any categories. Neither an animal nor a plant. Sadly, they have a bad reputation. You know, for some reason, I have always been fascinated by fungus from a very young age. My mother used to be so worried about me. I grew up in a remote town in Uttarakhand, where one easily comes across different varieties of mushrooms on a hike to the forest. Despite my mother's warning, when I got a chance—whenever she was off somewhere—I would cook the day's foraged mushrooms without thinking twice. I know, not a sensible thing to do, but I couldn't see any danger in them like the people around me. Even though they were a local delicacy, if one were to fall ill by mistakenly eating the poisonous ones, people avoided them all like the plague for some time," said Maya, dropping the little one into a cloth bag with the rest.

"Do you know this versatile fungus is also being used in sustainable waste management?" Maya asked, handing the bag to Juana.

"Really?" Juana wasn't sure if she'd heard her brother-in-law mentioning that.

"Yeah, because of their ability to break down compounds that prevent material from being degradable or recyclable."

Like a hawk, Maya's mushroom-hunter eyes scanned the dank forest floor. She pointed further ahead, and both moved towards it.

That night, Juana ate mushroom curry with rice, savoring the feel of the wild edible fungi she had foraged earlier. Some people hated the edible fungi for its rubbery, unnerving texture and earthy smell. It was one of the reason why mushrooms hadn't made it to her regular diet.

A sense of calm that had been eluding her for some time embraced her. The mushroom tasted, well, different. But it also tasted like the warmth of a mother's consolation, when one truly needed it.

Juana needed it. The past couple of days had, for some reason, made her acutely aware of her singleness and childlessness. In a world that privileged relationships and parenthood, she felt like an odd one. The feeling she had been immune to all these years!

Juana took another bite of her food and felt an intense kinship with the fungi she was eating. Being an anomaly in a world full of conformists isn't such a bad thing, Juana thought, especially if it enables you to live your true self.

......

Juana pulled over the car but remained seated for a moment. She had driven farther from where she and Maya had foraged for mushrooms the last time. The drizzle had been going on for over an hour. The sky looked like a sullen kid. She opened the car door and bared herself to the relentless fine drops falling from above.

Ignoring her sneakers soaking up the rain and muddying themselves blithely, her amateurish eyes scavenged the forest floor for any sign of edible fungi. The towering Sal trees offered minimal protection, as water gathered on their leaves dripped steadily onto the ground and her. The ground was covered with leaf litter. The fern, countless saplings, and ground plants growing in lush green covered the forest floor.

Despair. She wasn't as skillful a mushroom forager as Maya. It never took much time for Maya to spot mushrooms. It was as if some divine energy carried her exactly to the spot where mushrooms grew.

As time skittered by, Juana grew exasperated. Was she going to leave empty-handed? She was so sure of finding mushrooms immediately upon her arrival. She thought it was going to be easy and breezy. How wrong she was!

The thought of giving up was unbearable to her, but the darkening sky gave her no other choice. While returning to her parked car, Juana understood what people meant by saying disappointment can break hearts.

She climbed back into her car and drove off. While she was nursing her disappointment, Juana thought she spotted a solitary figure in the woods. Juana slammed on the brake. As she opened the car door and turned to where she saw the person, she realized it was the exact spot she and Maya had been at their last mushroom foraging trip. Juana scrambled to the spot.

As she approached, the figure traipsed further into the deep woods, then stopped and crouched on the ground. Juana remembered what Maya had once told her: much of the mushroom foraging in the world is done by women.

The woman turned to Juana and straightened. From her attire of *ghagra* and shirt blouse, she seemed to be an indigenous woman.

"Mushrooms?" Juana said.

As a response, the woman extended her right hand, and Juana gasped. With a texture like honeycomb, they were unmistakable.

The three morel mushrooms sitting in the woman's palm looked no less than diamonds. The morel mushrooms had historically proven difficult to be commercially cultivated and grew wild in India. Due to their rarity, they were the most prized mushroom variety, with sellers collecting up to 30,000 rupees per kg.

Juana couldn't help the wide grin spreading across her face. Maya would be so thrilled to see them, she thought.

After dropping the mushrooms into a jute basket by her feet, the woman crouched down again. That's when Juana followed the woman's eyes and gasped again.

They were few, but they were enough.

Looking slightly troubled, the woman turned to Juana, and then back to the fungi, and again to Juana. Juana moved closer and noticed the woman's hand hadn't moved towards the mushrooms. Juana understood the woman's quandary.

"I just need two. You can take the rest," she assured the woman. A smile of evident relief broke into the woman's face.

"They are very rare, aren't they?" Juana asked, without taking her eyes off the mushrooms.

"When I was a kid, morels were found in abundance. We could pick enough to cook some at home before selling the rest. But no longer. It's the early arrival of hot weather, you know? The availability of these mushrooms has decreased considerably over the past decades," the woman sighed.

The woman handed two mushrooms to Juana and deposited the rest she had plucked into her jute bag. Then she hauled herself up and wandered off, with her eyes planted down, likely searching for more morels.

With the scant natural light, Juana studied the two three-inch-tall edible fungi snugly sitting in her palm. Maya had once showed her a dry, tiny morel mushroom, but not a fresh one. The fragile conical caps, covered in irregular indentations, were gray, and the stems were pale cream. Gingerly, she circled her fingers over them, feeling their spongy touch. Drawing her hand to her nose, she took a deep inhale of their earthy smell.

Barely containing her excitement with the prospect of showing them to the sick Maya and seeing her eyes light up, Juana turned on her heel to drive to Maya's house when she noticed something. A tiny depression filled with water in the forest ground. Juana remembered seeing it the last time she and Maya were there. She swiftly turned to the spot of mushrooms, now bare and empty. The startling realisation that the mushrooms were exactly where the drunk was lying the last time knocked her sideways.

She felt a rush of tingling in her hand, and her hand shook momentarily. A part of her screamed to drop the mushrooms, but she didn't. Juana closed her eyes and took in a lungful of fresh forest air. Then she opened them, and without another glance at the dreadful spot, she hurried out of the woods.

***

5

WHEN IT RAINED

The looming trees stared down at her. Dhami glanced about. A whisper from inside told her she may not be alone after all. Her muscles tensed. The air was cool and still. Then, a noise akin to a shrill whistle shattered the quiet of the woods. She froze, forgetting to breathe for a moment. *Just a bird!* She tried to make sense. But the assurance did little to obliterate the growing unease. Dhami staggered back and lifted her hand to a tall deodar tree for support.

What am I doing here?

You wanted to try something new. To make yourself happy.

Is it working?

At the moment, no. It just backfired.

The familiar chatter in her mind calmed her. A rarity. A smile tore through her tightly pressed lips.

Venturing deep into the woods at dawn seemed adventurous when the idea prodded her the night before. But Dhami wasn't sure about it anymore. The tall deodar trees she found majestic in the bright daylight now disquieted her at the moment. The first rays of morning were slowly illuminating the area as she made her way out of the woods. As she emerged into the plain field, Dhami sighed with relief upon spotting three horses grazing at a distance. Another smile, wider, touched her lips.

Look at the lives around you, silly! Everything's alright. Dhami reassured herself.

Twenty minutes later, she entered the small cottage she had rented for two weeks in Dalhousie.

Dhami went straight to the kitchenette and made herself coffee. It'd been three days since she came to the hill station, and she had already explored the whole town. She took her coffee outside. Holding the cup with both hands and standing barefoot on the trimmed grass outside the cottage, Dhami gazed at the mighty Dhauladhar range on the horizon. She was glad she took her boyfriend's advice and made the trip to the hill station.

Over a month ago, one evening, she had gone to meet him at his house. He had asked her to come over since his mother was out shopping with her friend.

"Go," he had said, before slurping the last bit of soup in the bowl.

Despite enjoying her boyfriend's cooking, Dhami's appetite had suffered in recent days. She wasn't able to finish the soup but continued to eat it because it was made by him.

"Go where?" Dhami had asked.

Ijay placed his bowl on the table between them and leaned in to give his full attention to her.

"You decide that. But, think about it seriously. You really need a break from the mundane life that is draining you."

Dhami had stopped eating. It was not as if the thought hadn't crossed her mind countless times before. She believed that running away from one's life was something every human has wished for at some point. But, go where, and most importantly, how long should you stay gone? Something no one seemed to know for sure.

......

Dhami sprinted towards an oak tree as the rain began lashing the town. To her ill luck, the sparse canopy of the tree enabled the raindrops to sneak up on her, and their intensity quickly obscured her vision. Dhami cursed the timing. Then a muffled shout from close by caused her to glance around. A blurry figure of a tall man with a slight stoop stood on the veranda of a nearby house, waving her over. Dhami hesitated briefly before darting to the house. She climbed the steps of the veranda with an awkward smile.

"Why are you out now? Didn't you see the sky? Why aren't you carrying an umbrella? You are not from here, are you? No, no, otherwise you wouldn't be out now," the man said. Dhami shivered from the chill brought by the rain and the man's scrutinizing gaze.

"Oh, look at you! Come, come inside. I'll give you a towel to dry," the man suggested and began to turn.

An unknown fear jolted Dhami. "Oh, no, that's fine. Hopefully this rain will be over soon. I'll just wait here till then," she said hastily, and watched a frown appear on the man's face.

"No, you're not from here. You see, this rain is not stopping anytime soon. Come inside. I'll make some tea." The man didn't wait for her response and walked into his house. Despite her brain's warning to be cautious, the idea of holding something warm between her cold, shivering hands enticed Dhami. She looked over the darkened, wailing sky and warily walked into the house.

The first thing she noticed when stepping over the threshold was a sturdy antique table with an old vintage bronze and golden rotary dial telephone perched on it. She wasn't dripping, thankfully, but didn't have the heart to sit anywhere. Dhami's wary but curious eyes hovered over the black and white historical photos that were part of the decorations on the purple walls of the living room. The house didn't hit her as a colonial one, yet the floral upholstery and rustic designs gave it an old-world charm. Dhami looked at the rotary dial telephone again. She felt an itch to run her fingers on the dial.

"My wife was an obsessive collector of art and objects that inspired her."

Startled, Dhami almost jumped and turned to the voice. The man was holding a tray with two cups on it. He slightly bent his head towards the cup to his left and said, "This one is yours. I have less sugar in mine. I should have asked you about your sugar preference, but I assumed young people like sugary beverages and are less concerned about health than older folks like me."

Dhami forced a smile.

"Why aren't you seated? Oh, right, I should have brought you something to dry your head. Just sit anywhere. You're not that soaked to keep standing. Here, take this tea; I'll bring you a towel." The man held the tray towards her, and Dhami took the cup meant for her.

When the man placed the tray on the center table and was about to leave the room, Dhami said, "Don't worry about the towel. I'm kind of dry now."

The man eyed her wet hair glued to her head. "Are you sure?"

"Yes. Thanks for the tea," Dhami said, and the man waved his hand dismissively.

Dhami lowered herself on the edge of a wooden chair. The warmth of the cup against her cold skin felt good. Too good. The man took his cup and walked over to the salmon-pink lounge chair across from her.

"Where are you from?" the man asked after taking a sip of his tea.

"Pune."

Dhami despised such moments. Moments where strangers inquired about her life. The answers to them may be easy, but it always made her anxious for some reason.

"When did you come to Dalhousie?"

Dhami took a sip of her tea and relished the hot, sweet liquid seeping down her throat. "Five days ago."

"A solo traveler?"

Dhami smiled and nodded.

"My daughter also prefers to travel solo. Her partner is fed up with her."

"Where is she?"

"She doesn't live here. She lives in the Netherlands."

Dhami wondered about the man's wife.

"She was more attached to her mother," the man said, as if reading her thoughts. "My wife passed away two years ago." He turned his gaze to the three rose-coloured candles near the glass vase on the center table.

Dhami took three sips of the warm tea in succession. She didn't say anything.

Somewhere in the house a window banged shut. The whooshing sound of the wind outside disquieted her. Dhami was grateful for the large warm cup in her hand. It gave her comfort. She wished she was alone holding the hot beverage.

The man lifted his eyes off the candles and turned them to her. Dhami finished her tea but kept the cup in her hand.

"Did you explore the whole town? Did you like it?"

"Yes, I did."

The man nodded, took a sip, and looked up at the ceiling. Dhami followed his gaze and found nothing of interest.

"It's a small town but peaceful. A perfect place for soul seekers—that's what some people say. What do you do?"

"I'm a copywriter."

His eyes were back on her. "Oh," the man nodded. "How long are you in town?"

I don't know. I don't know anything.

"Just a couple more days."

The man replaced his cup on the tray and eyed the empty cup pressed between her hands. A sound of rattling from the upper floor diverted their eyes upward. Then they looked at each other.

"Why did you come in the off-season? You should have come next month. Do you enjoy snow?" he asked.

Dhami wasn't sure what to say. She'd never experienced snow, nor had she ever craved it. But since snow was something almost everyone seemed to enjoy, she nodded. "Yes."

"December to February are the best months to see snowfall. But only if you can tolerate extreme cold."

She couldn't. Dhami hated extremes: extreme cold or hot weather, extreme emotional reactions, extreme sadness, and the intense fear of the unknown.

Dhami rubbed her thumb against the smooth surface of the porcelain cup and felt a tiny bump near the handle.

......

She knew she was staring at the bump above his right eyebrow.

"Will you take your eyes off me?" Ijay sounded a bit exasperated.

The house fell quiet for a moment. They were, once again, alone in his house.

"What happened?" Dhami broke the silence.

"Bumped into my bedroom door."

Her eyebrows lifted. "Really?"

He peered into her eyes, expressionless. "Have you decided where you want to go?"

Dhami looked away, and her eyes landed on his guitar, gifted by his best friend, who was secretly in love with him. Dhami knew about it, but Ijay didn't. She hoped Ijay would never know.

"No, I haven't," she finally said, feeling his unwavering gaze on her.

"Say a letter."

She looked at him. "What?"

Again, a look of exasperation crossed his zit-covered face. "Just say a letter."

"D?"

"Another one."

"H?"

A smile cracked on his dry lips. "Dalhousie in Himachal Pradesh."

……

The rain continued to batter down.

"Where were you planning to go? Whatever your plans were for tonight, it's not possible now," the man said.

"Yeah, it seems that way," said Dhami.

Dhami had planned to eat out. She had planned to spend her time watching strangers and imagining their stories. She had planned to do something unusual. Something she could tell Ijay about. A tale to keep him interested in her. Moreover, she didn't feel like cooking dinner.

The man leaned forward, placing his forearms on his thighs and clasping his hands. "Where are you staying?" he asked.

Dhami told him, then flinched as a fierce clap of thunder resonated across the sky. When she looked back, the man had a woeful smile on his face.

Two blinks later, the smile vanished. "Have you encountered a Himalayan black bear? There was a time when they'd rarely be seen, but nowadays, many tourists and locals have reported seeing them."

Dhami shuddered and couldn't bring herself to respond. She suddenly recalled her early morning jaunt into the woods.

The woeful smile reappeared. "Don't worry. No one has been attacked by them so far. But they are unpredictable, so you must be careful when coming across one. Especially the mama bears. They're very protective of their young ones."

Mothers! Most mothers are protective and would do anything to keep their progeny safe. Ijay's mother was one of them. She didn't like Dhami. Dhami knew it. She also knew that Ijay knew that she knew. Sometimes she'd stay awake at night, imagining the conversations the mother-son duo had.

"Why her? There is something wrong with her! Hasn't she told you things that aren't true? She hears and sees things that don't exist. Why can't you have a normal girlfriend?" Ijay's mother would say in Dhami's mind.

Other times, to torture herself further, she'd imagine Ijay assuring his mother that he'd break up with her soon. Just the way her two ex-boyfriends did. There were no warning signs, and no explanations or reasons given later. They simply exited her life. Ijay was still in her life for eight months. But how long? How long would he ignore her mood swings and unrestrained emotions?

"I haven't seen them," Dhami said with a slight smile.

The man peered out of his front door and frowned. "Well, it's sad. The rain ruins all your plans." The man unclasped his hands and stared at his open palm. "How do you feel about rain?"

Dhami froze. She didn't take her eyes off the man, fearing that if she did, something unpleasant might happen. A sick feeling knotted her stomach. But it departed as soon as it came. The man looked up at her, and she realized she hadn't responded to his question.

How did she feel about the rain? The rain? Water droplets from the sky? How did Ijay feel about rain? Did he like it? Did she ever tell him that her second ex- boyfriend had broken up with her on a rainy day? Or was it the first ex? No, he had actually proposed to her on a rainy day. The first ex or the second ex? She couldn't remember correctly. Why was her memory all jumbled up? What would she tell Ijay?

"I think my boyfriend is going to break up with me soon. I don't want to go back because if I did, he'd ask me to meet and end our relationship."

The man's eyes bore into hers as he straightened in his seat. Then suddenly his shoulders slumped. Dhami realized her mistake.

What did I just say? Why did I say that? Why? The critters in her head chirped.

"I don't… I mean, I don't mind rain. Neither do I hate it, nor do I like it."

A moment of awkward silence ensued.

"But what if it ruins your plan?" The man tilted his head sideways.

The familiar fear percolated between her shoulder blades.

The man turned his solemn eyes to the internal staircase. "My father built this house according to vastu shastras, even this staircase. My wife fell from it one day and died. There was a leakage in the roof. It had been raining for three days. She slipped. Here. On these stairs, designed as per vastu shastra."

Dhami felt a warm tingling sensation around her left ear. Her breathing came out shallow and rapid. Her instincts told her something wasn't right with the man. Dhami looked at the cream ceiling, which looked waterproof to her. In her mind's eye, she could picture him pushing his wife down the stairs, checking her to make sure she was dead, and then crying crocodile tears.

"How did it ruin your plan? Wasn't it a perfect ploy?" Dhami said, turning to the man.

The man's attention slipped back to her, his eyes regarding her with confusion. "What?"

Dhami closed her eyes and shook her head like a parent expressing disapproval at her child's peccadilloes. She opened them to the perplexed look on the man's face. She knew she was looking at a killer. "How do you feel when you succeed in your plan?" she asked.

What if Ijay's mother succeeds in ending their relationship? What if Ijay learned his best friend was in love with him?

The man opened his mouth and closed it. He repeated it a few more times before he could form a sound. "I don't understand what you're trying to say."

The disapproving look on her face deepened. "Don't you? No, don't lie; you know what I mean."

The man swayed slightly forward. Suddenly, the walls in the house seemed to close in on her. A fleeting sensation of numbness was quickly replaced by a powerful wave of energy coursing through her limbs. Dhami dashed out of the house. The relentless downpour followed her every step. Twice, she almost got hit by oncoming vehicles. When she reached the safety of her cottage, soaked to the bone, she suddenly became aware of the weight in her right hand. Dhami looked down at her hand, still clutching the teacup. She released it, and the porcelain rose teacup crashed onto the wooden floor.

6

THE BLACK DOG

No one knew who the black dog belonged to. It wasn't a stray.

He had a collar. Black. Which looked chewed on close inspection. Could be the acts of other dogs. After all, he was a male dog. And males, irrespective of species, are predisposed to one thing: fighting.

Yes, I dared to approach him one afternoon while he was asleep. Not a wise thing to do, I realised. When I gingerly backed away, I could almost feel his eyes prodding my back.

No one had seen him. Like ever.

The people I talked to, three of them precisely, on my way to and from the music class, were locals. They were in their fifties and had lived their entire lives in our dreary town. According to them, they knew each and every human, critter, tree, and even weed on that small patch of land like the backs of their weathered hands. And none of them had seen a black dog anywhere in the area.

I never doubted them.. But I didn't doubt my eyes either. And my eyes saw what they saw. A black dog.

……

It was a brooding land. A patch of land devoid of any vegetation. Not even a single wispy blade of grass. It seemed to have worn its grab of desolation since the beginning of time. They said it was once a playground. Long, long ago. But they weren't sure about it. They actually heard it from others who heard it from others, and it went on and on. Although they weren't sure such a playground existed or not, they believed it might have existed during the British Raj. And that, they were sure of.

For the first time in my twenty-two years of life, I hated my introversion. I had no friend, no one to lug along to the music class and point to the dog from a safe distance and ask, 'Can you see a black dog like I do?'

It was a rugged terrain, severed from the tarmac road. I had to pass by the bare ground, supposedly a playground, to walk a little uphill to my music class.

After the initial few days, I was overcome with fascination by the dog.

Legends of black dogs were aplenty, mostly associated with the British and European countryside. Unlike the prim black domestic dogs, these creatures were sort of frightening and were very large, black, shaggy-coated, and often seen prowling the rural roads and town edges. Some stories described them as malevolent, as associates of witchcraft, or of the afterlife.

But I need not have had to worry, as the black dog in the playground was neither intimidatingly large nor shaggy-coated.

It was just a medium-sized, lean-bodied black dog, with a grim demeanor and baleful eyes.

I shared my thoughts with one of my acquaintances.

"I mean, some people carry dark energy with them. The Britishers, well, they weren't good folks, were they?" He was weeding around a plant with purple flowers outside his house fence. Despite setting aside all the plucked weeds on the soil, he remained crouched.

"You think the dog is a ghost or some sort of malevolent entity?" I asked.

He stared into the distance, either at clumps of small houses like his own jutting out of the land or at the cloudless sky, which looked like a vast placid ocean.

"Why, then, no one has seen it except you?" He didn't turn to me and, thankfully, didn't see my reaction.

"We don't know if anyone else has seen it or not. I mean, I have talked to only three people, including you. Someone must have seen it other than me. And, why me?"

The idea of the black dog being phantasmal wasn't exactly enticing to me.

I began moving. "I should go."

"How are your violin lessons going?" He twisted his neck, still crouched, to face me.

I had been dreading the question.

I hesitated. "Not that great. Actually—

"You're not exactly into it," he completed what I might not have said.

"Then why not give up?" He looked genuinely perplexed.

A whiff of ripe guava tickled my nostrils. Weird, since there were no guava trees around.

"My aunt and uncle wouldn't like that. My dad was really into music, especially violin. Wanted to make a career as a violin teacher even though he wasn't exactly good at it. He ended up being an accountant. When my parents were alive, he encouraged me to learn violin. And I wasn't interested in it. I kept putting it off. Then he and Mama passed away. My uncle believes I should learn violin, as my father would have wanted me to."

"Does he know that you don't enjoy playing the violin?"

I shifted from one foot to another but didn't say anything. He understood.

"They don't know, do they? Lack of communication can be detrimental to relationships. That's the reason, I was told, my first wife left me."

......

I watched him from a distance. I left the music class earlier, complaining about a stomachache that didn't exist. I bluffed myself that he hadn't seen me come down the narrow path, immediately skirt to a tree, and hide behind it. He was sniffing the bare ground. What did he eat to survive? A part of me wished I had something to feed him; another part wondered if phantom dogs even got hungry. Then there was a third part, a timid, scared one, who wouldn't dare approach anyone with malicious eyes, be it a human or an animal.

The dog curled up on the ground with his back to me, when suddenly I realized that I could snap his picture. I fumbled into my bag and dug out my phone and looked at him. He was sitting on his haunches now, looking into the distance. I followed his eyes and listened. It was faint at first, a low grumble, then a thunderous noise shook the sky, jolting me. My disbelieving eyes watched a dark, swirling mass on the horizon, rising rapidly and expanding as it rolled towards me. I was dumbfounded. The sky hadn't portended rain. I prepared to leave, but, first, I had to quickly take a picture of the dog. When I looked back at the dog, I almost shrieked, finding him staring at me.

Maybe he sensed my fear, or maybe he was distracted by a bird's call and looked away, and I, like a stealthy cat, took the opportunity to scamper out of there.

......

The woman looked at me like a principal looking at a delinquent student. The rain showed me no mercy. Beads of rainwater dripped from my hair and chin onto her living room floor. I flashed an apologetic smile. She vanished into the dark hallway and came out holding a bathing towel.

The dark clouds hadn't wasted any time in bathing the world in a mournful gray. The woman had closed the front door after ushering me in. The interior of the house was no different from the world outside. The depressingly dark living room was devoid of any decorative items. I had never been inside the house in my three months of being acquainted with the woman.

My eyes danced around. Soot, an iron skillet, Raven, and my late mother's tar-black hair came to mind when looking around the living room. The bleakness of the room was dense, like viscous lava.

Handing me the towel, she gestured to dry my hair, whether out of concern for me or to keep her floor from getting wet than it already was.

She looked impatient, like she always did. Her slightly puckered face was immutable, no matter what the time of day was.

I shivered, and she reluctantly offered me a plastic chair to sit on.

"I wasn't expecting it," I said, referring to the rain.

A crackle followed by a faint rumbling from the sky above interjected.

The woman drew in a deep breath and sat on an armchair opposite to me.

"Isn't everything about life unpredictable?" She said, ostensibly not expecting an answer from me.

She didn't turn on the light, and we relied only on the faint light leaking through the shut glass window. Her eyes were on them as she continued.

"When I was young, I was so naive I believed that the right action always gave us desired results. Study well, get good grades. Work hard, earn wealth and success. Pray for the husband's safe return or his mental stability, and everything will be well. How stupid was I!"

Oh, right, her husband. She had mentioned him in passing once. Wasn't he a sailor or something who got lost while working on a cargo ship?

I wasn't really interested, but unfortunately the drumming on the roof suggested the rain had no intention of stopping.

So I asked, "What happened?"

She shot me a furtive glance, then her eyes were back on the window.

She didn't respond. I remained mum. The rain continued.

Then, "Did you see your dog today?" She was looking at me.

The change of subject threw me off guard. My dog? The black dog!

Yes, I did. What should I say? The truth?

"No, I didn't," I lied. It was better that way.

"Maybe it went back to where it came from. Didn't I say this to you the first day? Probably a runaway dog."

She was one of the three people I talked to about the black dog.

Suddenly her brows reached for each other. "How strange! Even my husband wanted a dog. A black one. He said in Vedic astrology the black dog symbolises protection, and feeding one regularly helps in warding off negative energy from home. But we never had one. I was against it. It was mostly after he returned from the sea. He'd talk about getting a dog. I'd dissuade him. Then he'd drop the subject. Then he'd be off to sea again. And he'd return home talking about getting a dog. It went on like this for many years. Maybe if we had a child, he might have been fulfilled. Or maybe we should have just gotten a black dog."

Birds called out from somewhere, and I was suddenly aware of the lack of sound of rain. As if reading my mind, the lady stood and opened the front door, and natural light rushed in.

"I talked to two of my husband's friends, who worked with him on the same cargo ship. Something was happening to him. To my husband. Months before he was lost to the sea, he was very morose at home. Would barely talk and snapped at everything. They saw the changes in him too. His friends. They said it was especially at night when his mood dropped. He would seem entranced by the sea and stare at the blackness below. Every night. Could you imagine what the sea looked like at night? Utter blackness and mystery."

The bird calls were getting louder and mellifluous. Life always resumed after torrential rain.

The woman held my eyes with a befuddled look on her face. "He was there one moment, staring at the sea at night, and gone the next morning. His body was never found. Was it an accident, or—? What was he looking at? It's been five years, and yet I cannot stop asking myself, 'What was he looking at in the dark sea?"

I stepped outside the house and clomped back to my uncle's house.

……

He shrieked, grunted, and mocked her by mimicking her accusations. He was good at it. Of course, one would get good at something they did day after day. The house fell silent. Briefly. An unversed person might mistake it for over. But I knew better.

She was saying something. Quietly. Probably to keep me from overhearing. But why try? I knew everything. About the other woman in my uncle's life. Whenever she accused him of having an affair, he either deflected or mocked her by imitating her in a silly, juvenile manner.

Something clattered. Probably a vessel. More murmurings followed, then growls of frustration from my uncle. Thumping sounds. Probably my aunt banging her hands on the dining table, her patience thinning with each strike.

In a voice that sounded like a squeaking mouse, my aunt said something.

I just couldn't understand my uncle. Why couldn't he just admit to having an affair? It's not as if my aunt would leave him after his confession. It was tragically comic at this point. The wife knew her husband was having an affair, and the husband knew that the wife knew he was having an affair, and yet he wasn't admitting it. What was the point of holding back the truth?

"Stop. Stop. Stop saying that. I have seen her, okay? Why did you lie about being with your friend last Thursday?" My aunt sounded hysterical.

Of course she wasn't going to get any sincere truth from him. A part of me was disgusted at her fruitless attempts to make my uncle admit. She wasn't going to leave him and was going to continue to live with him despite the truth. Then why bother?

"Meh. Meh. Meh. Meh. Mehh!" My uncle mocked, disparagingly, as usual.

As per his custom, my uncle would either storm into a room used as his home office, where several books on the bookshelf were about relationships, or storm out of the house. I listened. The front door banged shut. I couldn't stop smiling. The front door always remained open during the day, and he had no reason to slam it closed. But, then, how would he show his frustration?

My mind went to the one who should actually be frustrated and mad.

I opened the door and padded to the dining room. With a slight scowl on her face, she wiped the already sparkling table clean.

"I'll help you with dinner tonight," I said.

Her hand paused briefly, then resumed. She gave an imperceptible nod, without meeting my eyes.

She usually kept me away from the kitchen, but on days like this, when a fight happened, she wouldn't refuse my offer to help her in the kitchen.

……

My music teacher seemed to have had enough of me. He couldn't conceal his bafflement at my lackadaisical manner of playing the violin. It was clear to him that my heart wasn't into it.

Yes, unlike other days, I failed to mask my true feelings, and I blame it on the black dog.

Where was he? Was he truly a ghost? A fabrication of my imagination? I hadn't seen him for four days. Maybe I shouldn't have tried to take his picture. Maybe he didn't like that.

The radiant, azure midday sky grinned at me as I stepped out of my music teacher's house.

My heavy heart protested against walking fast. I didn't want to go to my uncle's house.

Maybe I'd be lucky to meet one of my three acquaintances, and maybe, they'd take pity on me and engage me with some tall tales.

While I was thinking about my acquaintance with a runaway first wife, another with a lost husband at sea, and the third who mostly looked back at his youthful idealism and lamented his disappointed hopes, I saw something dart to the corner of my periphery, causing me to turn my head in surprise.

There he was, casually sauntering on the ground. My heart wasn't excited at his sudden appearance and began pacing. Where had he come from? My fear froze me. I was just a few meters from him, and yet he didn't look at me. He paused, sniffed the soulless dusty ground, and looked up to stare ahead into the distance. I followed his eyes and found nothing there. When I turned to him, he was curled up with his back to me. His eerie quickness never failed to unnerve me.

But I finally found my opportunity. So setting aside my own uneasiness, I captured him in my phone's camera.

……

He was standing outside his house, his Golden Retriever by his side, and both were looking at a woman seemingly charging towards the large metal trash bin.

His face scrunched when the woman flung the trash in her hand, aiming for the bin from a distance, and missing the target. He looked away, disgusted, and happened to see me coming.

I usually avoided him, as he talked too much, a trait I despised in fellow humans. Sometimes I wondered if garrulous people talked too much because they liked hearing their own voices.

His Golden Retriever's tail wagged maniacally on seeing me. It was because of his lab that I first approached him, asking if the black dog was also his.

"Hi, Missy," I addressed the dog, and her human companion looked pleased with my conversation opener.

"How are your violin lessons going?" he asked. I hated when people asked me that.

I looked at him, patting the head of Missy, and loving the softness of her fur on my dry skin. I nodded and managed a very awkward smile.

He didn't say anything immediately, surprising me. Probably half a minute passed in utter silence, which he broke by saying, "It's not easy, you know? Music lessons. My niece plays piano beautifully and teaches it, but that is because she'd been playing it since she was five. See, I'm not saying you can't learn to play musical instruments at your age or at any age, but to be really good at it can be difficult if you haven't started it at a very young age."

I repressed a sigh. He definitely misinterpreted my nonverbal cue.

"It's not for everyone. Seeing how well my niece played, I encouraged my daughter to learn as well, but she didn't enjoy it. She was a very stubborn kid."

"It's nice you didn't force her to do something she didn't like. Some parents fail to understand that their children aren't the exact mold of them. They don't see their children as individuals with different dreams, passions and ambitions."

The man pursed his lips, displeased with my remark. Probably he was hoping I would take pity on him for having had to raise a difficult child.

Missy had started circling around me with her smiley face. She made me laugh that day.

"Do you still see that black dog you asked me about?" He asked.

"Yeah, he's still there," I said, taking a brief break from patting Missy, which she complained about by thrusting her nose against my hand.

"God knows how the dog is surviving if it is still there. I mean, I haven't seen a black dog anywhere here, and there are no houses near the playground, so what was the dog surviving on?"

That was a puzzle I hadn't solved yet.

"Is your dog dark brown or like black black? I know someone, Mr. Joshi; he owns that big grocery near that dental clinic. You might have seen that grocery. And the dental clinic. My friend owns that dental clinic. We've known each other since college. Oh, so the grocery store—no, no, Mr. Joshi had a dog, a brown one, you know, like that chocolate colour, and one day on one of his walks, the dog wandered off somewhere or something, I'm not sure, and they couldn't find it."

Suddenly I remembered taking the black dog's photo. So I pulled out my phone from my jeans pocket and showed the photo to him.

He put his face close to my phone, then turned to me with a scowl, simultaneously leaning his head back.

"I may look old to you, but my eyes are still strong, thanks to God's grace."

I began to feel woozy. Something about his expression and remark wasn't sitting right with my expectations.

"What do you mean?" I asked.

"That's a big rock and not a dog."

I pulled my hand back and looked. I thought I'd faint any moment. There was a large rock in the photo. I had taken a picture of a large rock.

Suddenly, going to my uncle's house wasn't less enticing.

Without saying a word or looking at the man, I shoved my phone into my jeans pocket and jogged to my uncle's house.

7

PEACOCK CALLS

He awoke to the peacock calls piercing the jungle's silence. The towering tree canopies obscured his view of the sky. Tamal felt disoriented. He didn't know where he was. His head snapped around as fear crept up his spine. Then a voice whispered "*You're in a forest.*" Tamal had no idea how he ended up in a forest. As he tried to recall, the scene around him began shifting. Blinding white clouds enveloped him and carried him skyward. Tamal tried to scream.

The dream flickered out as Tamal opened his sleepy eyes. He turned to his other side and was hit by the boisterous laughs of his housemates from outside his room. Tamal hated the moment. If given a choice, he would never get out of his bed. The bed itself wasn't comfy, with a thin mattress and a hard pillow, but it definitely was a source of comfort to Tamal. Almost always the moment he hit his head on the pillow, he was taken on a tour of dreamland. The real world didn't hold any charm for him.

Reluctantly, he tossed his legs off the bed and listened. The apartment was quiet. Tamal didn't hate his housemates but couldn't bring himself to like them either. They were too peppy and exuberant for his taste. He thought they were fake. He didn't believe that anyone could be ebullient all the time. It just wasn't possible.

But most preferred the company of people like his housemates. No one liked spending time with people like Tamal. His own parents preferred his friends' company whenever they came over to visit. Tamal couldn't care less. In fact, that was exactly how he liked it — to be left alone! But not all the time. And even when he wanted company, it would be of like-minded people. Unfortunately, he never met anyone who had the same interest or demeanor as him. Except for *her*.

Tamal opened the drawer on the bedside table and took his phone out. He hated keeping his phone on the bed with him. In the darkness of the night, he liked to believe that he was alone, without any responsibilities and worries in the world. His phone had the potential to burst that illusion, so he kept it away from him.

The city was closed due to protests involving two warring communities. Tamal searched the internet to find out if the protest was peaceful or had devolved into violence. Peaceful protests were very rare to witness. As of then, there had been no fatalities or damage to vehicles. Let's see how long it stayed that way, Tamal thought.

There were two missed calls from his mother the night before. She might have learned about the protest on the news and gotten worried. Suddenly, a memory sparked in his mind.

Tamal's mother was watering the plants in the courtyard, while his father read aloud a series of newspaper headlines that either captured his interest or amused him. Starting with reports of crimes and human-caused environmental degradation, he ended it with a story of a government school kid inventing a solution for an eco-friendly air purifier.

Tamal's mother, a former history teacher well-versed in human brutality, remarked, "We humans consider ourselves superior to other beings, and yet, we prove ourselves wrong every time. We fight, we kill. We commit horrendous crimes. We don't even spare our own people. It's as if some of us need just any excuse to harm others." A scowl marred her usually serene face as she moved a water hose from one plant to another. Standing by the doorway with his tea, Tamal saw it first and braced for its impact.

His father's dismissive laughter was not surprising, but that didn't make it less hurtful. Tamal's mother didn't turn to her husband or react, but Tamal could almost feel her annoyance wafting from her.

Tamal had always been cautious of what he said to others, afraid of their reactions. Disagreement he could handle, but condescension, he couldn't. So, from a young age he kept his opinions to himself. But that changed when he met *her*.

……

She was the elder daughter of the neighbor. He rarely saw her growing up, as she attended a boarding school and later relocated to another city to live with relatives while studying for her wildlife science degree.

He remembered vividly that it was not him, but her, who made the first move. As usual, he was intoxicated in her presence. She was sitting close to him, seemingly listening to his gibberish. He no longer remembered what nonsense he was spewing out at that moment. It was hard not to lose himself in her presence. He was sure she knew the hold she had on him. While his wild ideas about life were tumbling out of his mouth, she leaned closer and kissed him on his cheek. He froze. He turned to her. Her flirtatious smile beckoned him. He leaned forward to kiss her, but she turned away and raised her chin sideways. He followed her gesture and was disheartened to see a few people behind them on the beach.

......

It was drizzling when he left his office one evening. By the time he reached home, he was soaked. He was quick to notice his neighbor's house shimmering with decorative lights. Most years, the decorative lights remained unlit except for special occasions or festivals. Since no festival was around the corner, he presumed something special was happening there. His mother told him about Nyra.

"You don't remember her, do you? Well, you were small, probably 8 or 9 years old, when she was sent to boarding school. She works in…"

"Works in?" His mother was serving him dinner. Tamal scooped bitter gourd curry with his roti and brought it to his mouth.

His mother pulled a chair next to him and sat on it. She looked contemplative briefly, then her face lit up, and she almost shouted, "Wildlife biologist! She told me she's a wildlife biologist and works in Dehradun. She's just visiting her family."

"Oh. Papa had his dinner?"

"You know how he is sometimes. At 6 pm, when I was watching my show, he started whining that he was hungry. I had to cook very fast."

......

Two days later, in the morning, when he saw her giving him a sweet, friendly smile and a wave, he froze. Throughout the day, in his office, he berated himself mercilessly for acting weird. That evening, he asked his mother about Nyra's marital status. He glanced at his father watching TV in the living room to make sure he couldn't hear them. His mother threw him a look that he couldn't decipher.

"She's divorced."

Tamal wasn't expecting that at all. His curiosity jumped tenfold. He asked his two friends, Jyoti, who was also Nyra's cousin, and Kartik, to hang out with him the coming Sunday evening.

When they met in their favorite cafe, Tamal didn't waste any time and jumped directly to the subject fermenting in his head.

"Your cousin is divorced," he stated, once the waiter left with their order.

Kartik and Jyoti ogled at him with surprise. He was not the kind of person who poked at others' personal matters.

"Yeah, she is," said Jyoti.

"Why?"

With furrowed eyes, she studied his face as if ensuring that he was the same Tamal she had been friends with.

"Well, she no longer wanted to live with her ex." When Tamal opened his mouth again, she cut him off, "I know, you want to know 'why.' Well, Nyra believed her ex didn't treat her as an equal. She was stressed and overworked. Not only did she work six days a week but also had to handle all the house chores on her own. Her ex never helped her, even when she felt overwhelmed. Her in-laws never supported her and often compared her with other married working women who also managed the house without any complaint. It diminished her self-worth."

"So she divorced her husband just because he didn't help her with house chores? Is that a good reason to end a relationship? My sister-in-law is also a working woman, but she also assists my mom with house chores," said Kartik.

"What about the men in your house?"

Kartik opened his mouth, then closed it.

A look of disapproval crinkled Jyoti's face. "I don't know why you treat your sister-in-law the way you do, but, yes, it is a good reason to end a relationship. If your partner treats you like a machine, then you're better off. When would men realise that house chores are not just a women's responsibility?"

Tamal cursed himself for voicing his curiosity. He didn't want his friends to argue or fight.

At the nearby table, an elderly couple sat, evidently enjoying the evening and their meal. With a blissful smile gracing her face, the lady was leaning over the table, listening to the man sitting across from her. Tamal imagined his father and mother as the couple, only to find it utterly laughable.

......

They drove in silence for the majority of the journey. Tamal kept glancing at her to gauge her mood. To an unfamiliar eye, she seemed calm and composed. But Tamal sensed her unease. He hoped he wasn't making a mistake. The city now lay behind them, its blurred lights in the far distance.

"What happened? Not curious to know where we're going?" Tamal asked.

She didn't look at him. "I asked you once, but you didn't tell me."

His heart sank at her cold response, but Tamal didn't allow it to cloud his mood.

That, however, didn't stop the bubbles of unease from forming within him, and he almost cried with joy as a lone building appeared in his view. He turned to the dirt path leading to the building and cut the engine.

Except for a streetlight at a distance, darkness wrapped their surroundings. She turned to him.

"It's a college building under construction," he said.

"And why are we here?" she asked, with her usual playful smile. Tamal felt at ease at once.

They opened their doors and stepped out of the car. He took her hand. She didn't ask any questions and allowed him to lead her. The sense of dread reappeared. Her hand was limp in his; she didn't hold him back, the way she usually did.

With his mobile's flashlight, he led her to the terrace of the building. He didn't let go of her hand. He could feel that something wasn't right.

Tamal worried when she gently pulled her hand from his and walked towards the parapet wall. Just as the stars overhead twinkled, the city lights glimmered on the horizon. They watched in silence for a minute, then Tamal turned to her. Again, he took her hand into his, prompting her to look at him. She had a distant look in her eyes. Her lips didn't elicit a smile.

"Nyra, you know how I feel about you, and I know you feel the same for me. We've been seeing each other for three months now, and I think it's the right time for me to ask you—Nyra, will you marry me?"

The look in her eyes seesawed between pity and disappointment.

"Tamal, I don't…."

Tamal cut her off, fearing the worst. "Nyra, I know you probably lost faith in marriage. Maybe you fear I'd turn out to be like your ex-husband. Trust me, I'll not be a douche like your ex. I love you; you know that, right? Then, how can I hurt or disappoint you? I'll never do anything to upset you. I know some—oh, no, most—take their spouse for granted, but I won't. If it's about the house chores, then I'll help you with everything. Like I said, I love you. I'll do anything to make you happy."

Nyra inched towards him and placed her left hand on his right cheek, making his heart skip a beat.

"I can't, Tamal. I'm sorry."

The rushing of emotions smothered his voice, and he managed to whisper, "But, why?"

The high-pitched sound of the peacock came from the pitch-black wilderness behind them. Nyra turned to the sound, and then her eyes were back on him.

"I don't know."

……

For a month, Tamal barely talked to his family. His mother didn't question him. A week after the rejection, on a Saturday evening, his mother entered his room. He didn't acknowledge her presence, hoping it would drive her away. She stood close to him and briefly joined him in staring out of his bedroom window. After two minutes of silence, she gave him a kiss on his head and walked out of his room. Tamal's eyes teared up.

It's been a year since he saw Nyra. A month after the rejection, she went back to Dehradun. He tried once to change her mind, but her answer remained the same. Four months later, he applied for a job in another city.

......

Only recently, Tamal discovered his disdain for the peacock. He knew his hatred for the peacock was unreasonable and childish. But to him, the peacock's cries appeared to mock him for the rejection he faced that evening. It was a ludicrous thought. A few days ago, while watching TV with his housemates, he found himself getting angrier as a peacock danced and tried to woo a peahen. He almost shouted to the peacock, *"Can't you see, she's not into you?"*

Perhaps he was scowling because one of his housemates asked him if he was alright, and said that he looked kind of mad.

Tamal's eyes crinkled as he formed a fake but believable smile on his face. His friends were discussing something about the peacock, and all Tamal wanted was to scream at them to change the channel, and if they didn't, punch them, then get inside the TV and punch the vain peacock.

The peacock also reminded him of his father. The way he patronized his mother.

"You know peacocks can fly," said his housemate, Daksh.

It was getting difficult to suppress his annoyance any longer. He closed his eyes and remembered what Nyra had said when the loud screaming of the peacock continued till they left the building on the night of his rejection.

"It either senses danger or is looking for a peahen."

Tamal was too heartbroken to care about a peacock's distress.

It'd been a year, and yet, he couldn't stop thinking about her. He hated her, and he hated himself for hating her. But he couldn't shake off feeling like a school kid getting the report card and finding out that all his classmates and friends had passed except him.

......

Tamal woke up with a nasty headache and was relieved to learn that his office was still closed, as the protest from the day before had turned violent and ugly by nightfall, and it wasn't safe to step outside.

He chatted with his housemates while preparing his breakfast and called his mother and assured her that he was fine. He had sent a message to both his parents the night before, but that wasn't enough for his mother. Her reply was to call him first thing in the morning. After ending the call, for some odd reason, his mind pulled him back to the past.

Two months after Nyra's arrival, they'd gone to the oldest cafe in their town. She chatted with the owner, who was good friends with her parents and had last seen her when she was a child. Minutes later, the amiable owner left them alone and they placed their order. Despite being a neighbor, Tamal had no memory of her as a child. She went to boarding school when she was 12, so that would make him 9 at that time. Why didn't he remember anything about her? Did they ever play?

She pondered over the question, "I think we did."

"Why didn't you ever visit during vacations?" Tamal wondered aloud.

"Who said I didn't? I visited twice—oh no, thrice actually. Your family would be off somewhere during those visits."

"Yeah, we'd visit my grandparents and relatives in Andhra Pradesh. But why only thrice?"

Nyra looked away, and a distant look appeared in her eyes. She turned to him, "I don't get along with my stepmother. I mean, we don't hate each other, but..." She trailed off, and Tamal nodded in understanding.

"I'd spend my vacations at my maternal grandmother's house or with my relatives. Sometimes my family would visit me there. That is why we never saw each other all these years."

The twinkle in her eyes, accentuated by the gentle glow of the cafe, made it nearly impossible for Tamal to look away. When they were about to leave, it was drizzling outside. They decided to wait, hoping the drizzle would subside. A mistake. The drizzle drew up volume, and the rain confined them to the cafe for another hour.

As they watched the rain misting the world outside, Tamal felt a light touch on his shoulder. He turned and peered into the eyes of Nyra.

She leaned closer and whispered, "Have you ever seen a peacock dance in the rain?"

……

Memories—that's what remained in the end.

"Hey, have you ever seen a peacock dance in the rain?"

Tamal's jaw went slack, and he looked puzzled.

Daksh was grinning. Tamal's other housemate, Parth, smacked the back of Daksh's head. Daksh glowered at him.

"Peahen, you dumb, not peacock," Parth corrected him.

Tamal's puzzled look remained intact, causing his housemates to laugh at him. Tamal closed his mouth and followed his housemates as they left his room, gesturing to follow them.

They looked out of Parth's bedroom balcony at a neighbor's terrace. A young woman, who seemed to be in her thirties, was dancing in the rain.

"See, that's a peahen, not a peacock," Parth said, seemingly proud of himself.

Daksh gave his characteristic boisterous laugh and said, "Have you ever seen a beautiful peahen? No! Because peahens aren't as beautiful as their male counterparts. Peacocks are beautiful and dazzling, and she, my boys, is a peacock to me."

Parth shook his head, and Tamal let out a hearty laugh.

The woman kept dancing in the rain, oblivious to the three men watching her.

8

MASHAKA, THE EVIL HAND

She recoiled. The tail came right off in her hand. The lizard escaped.

The lizard's detached tail, pressed between her left hand's thumb and index finger, wiggled. She willed her left hand to drop the detached tail, but it didn't comply. From the peach-coloured wall, the stupefied house lizard looked at her with beady eyes. To Tara, the lizard appeared to be trying to understand why she had suddenly attacked it for no reason. The house lizard had been living with her for five months, and never had she shown any kind of hostility towards it. Until now.

"I'm sorry. I didn't mean to," Tara mumbled to the lizard. Perhaps distrusting her, the lizard scurried towards the ceiling.

In her hand, its detached tail stopped wiggling. Her left hand finally dropped it.

Distressed, she felt a strong urge to call her mother and pour her heart out but decided against it.

As if unperturbed, and to augment Tara's distress, her left hand began to levitate. With her right hand, Tara brought it back to her side.

It all started after her brain surgery a year ago. Since then her left hand sort of became a foreign thing to her. It sprouted a mind and will of its own.

Alien hand syndrome! That's what her doctor told her.

Some days it was hard to live with her left hand. It grabbed objects she had no intention of touching, lifted itself up and then down repeatedly at random times, earning her puzzled looks from onlookers. When she would pull open any drawer, her left hand would immediately slam it shut. Most days it was uncooperative. It made Tara anxious, especially in her workplace. Her left hand had deliberately dropped her computer mouse thrice, poked the head of a coworker she didn't like, begun drumming on the table during an enervating meeting before Tara's right hand grabbed it and pinned it on her lap, tossed a notepad of a coworker under the table of another while they were having lunch in the canteen. But unlike other days, Tara couldn't allow it to ruin her day.

Tara had invited her new boyfriend to her apartment. When she tried a different hairstyle a few minutes ago, her left hand messed it up. But, unlike other days, Tara didn't lose her patience. She had promised herself that she wouldn't allow Mashaka to ruin her day. Yes, she referred to her left hand as 'Mashaka,' a term derived from African roots that translates to 'the troublemaker.'

The doorbell broke her trance. Tara washed her hands and rushed to open the door.

......

She handed him spiced tea and sat closer to him on the sofa. He smelled of cedar wood and citrus, igniting a childhood memory of visiting Himachal Pradesh with her parents and relishing a citrus fruit locally known as Kimb.

"Are you sure you're not hungry?" she asked, her eyes briefly running over the mole on his upper lip. She had read somewhere that a mole on the upper lip predicts a person's success in their career, and on the lower lip, success in their romantic relationship. Tara wished she had a mole on her lower lip.

Her current boyfriend, Edhas, shook his head. "I had breakfast late. Let's wait for an hour, then we'll eat. But if you're hungry, we can eat now."

She wasn't. She was too excited to be with him to care about food. "No, that's fine. We can eat whenever you feel like it."

Mashaka began to levitate, but Tara grabbed it swiftly with her right hand and kept it pressed on her lap. Her heart began to panic. She studied her boyfriend's face, which showed no change in expression. He sipped his tea and smiled. Tara's tense body relaxed.

"Why aren't you having tea with me?" Edhas asked. The smirk on his face indicated that he knew the answer already.

"I'm cutting down on my caffeine intake. It is disrupting my sleep." Yes, it was disrupting her sleep as well as expanding her waistline. She put lots of sugar in her hot beverages, without which she couldn't enjoy them, and, due to that, her clothes were getting tighter.

......

She couldn't believe she was having a great time with her new boyfriend. They had been together for just a month, and it was the first time they were spending any real quality time together.

Tara felt euphoric. Hope fired up within her. Maybe, she could make it work. Maybe, he was the one for her.

"Wow, this tofu fried rice tastes so good, Tara. And this kheer," Edhas said, taking a spoonful of it into his mouth. Tara grinned and gave a blissful sigh.

Edhas was known for his avuncular charm among the interns in their workplace. Tara had developed a strong crush on him three months back. She was ecstatic the day she learned he had feelings for her too.

She watched as Edhas's delighted face turned into a frown, which soon morphed into a grimace as he pulled out a two-inch-long hair from his mouth.

Appalled and mortified, Tara's breathing stilled briefly. She fumbled for words. "I, oh God, I don't understand how… Let me bring you another one." She sprang to her feet.

"That's fine, Tara." Edhas flashed her a fake smile and nudged the bowl of *kheer* away from him. He turned his head, his eyes falling on the succulents on the windowsill.

Her heart plummeted. Was he regretting coming to her house? Tara tortured herself with the thought.

They ate in silence till her left hand began to drum on the table. Tara closed her eyes and pleaded with her left hand internally to stop drumming. But obeying Tara was not its forte.

Edhas's frown reappeared. But he managed a perplexed grin and lifted a glass of water before him. He took a sip, and his frown deepened. Her left hand's fingers were snapping. A sickening feeling grew in Tara's stomach.

"What? Why are you doing that?" Edhas asked with confusion.

Tara must have looked awful, for Edhas studied her face, growing concerned.

"Are you okay, Tara?" he asked.

Tara gulped. "Yeah, I am," her voice came out weakly. Edhas pressed his lips together, looking unconvinced.

"Could I have some more water?" he requested, tilting his empty glass.

Tara shot up from her seat and dashed to her kitchen. She avoided looking at her left hand. She was shaking with fury and embarrassment.

With a trembling hand, she held a glass to Edhas and took her seat.

"Are you sure you're okay, Tara?" Edhas asked.

Tara nodded, mouthing a soft yes.

"Okay. If there's anything, you can tell me. You look kinda stressed."

Tell him. Tell him! Her mind screeched. *Tell him it's your damn hand!* Tara ignored it. Her past experiences had taught her not to overshare her personal problems with romantic partners. It pushed them away.

Before she could say anything, Mashaka began to levitate.

......

A sob racked her chest. Edhas had left her apartment five minutes ago.

Tara smacked her right palm on the kitchen counter. An angry hot tear fell from Tara's eyes, and her trembling right hand lifted to point an accusing finger at it._

"Enough is enough!" Tara hissed.

Mashaka ignored her and began drumming on the kitchen counter.

"You witch! You're trying to ruin my relationship with Edhas. You want him to ditch me. You want him to think I'm crazy, just the way you did with my previous boyfriends!" Tara raged.

Mashaka stopped drumming. Tara could almost hear Mashaka saying…

Your first boyfriend cheated on you with your friend. It is not my fault.

"How dare you! It was you who made him believe I'm a weirdo!" Tara accused, struggling to control her fury.

If that's what you want to believe. Your second boyfriend, or lover, was a married man with two children. It is not my fault that he got tired of you and moved on to his new interest. It is not my fault. Nope, no, not my fault!

Tara sniffed, wiping at her nose. She had seen it coming. When he had stopped answering her calls, and when they were together, he stopped kissing her affectionately the way he used to in the beginning of their relationship. He began to leave within fifteen minutes of arriving at her place, making excuses about his wife and children. He commenced pointing out her unflattering physical traits, which he had overlooked for more than a year. He smiled less and frowned more. Until one day, she could take it no more. An argument erupted, and he ended their relationship. Before he walked out the door, his face contorted with distaste as he spat, "You're a crazy woman, you know that?"

Stunned and hurt, Tara froze. Then a surge of rage shook her. But no retort came out of her. There was a drop of truth in what he said, wasn't there? Mashaka had made her look crazy many times, drawing perplexed looks from him.

"Why? Why do you have to make my life hard?" Tara protested.

Like mother, like daughter. Mashaka showed no change of heart.

At once, all sounds faded away, leaving only the muted shrill howling within her.

Tara grabbed her left wrist with her right hand. "How dare you! How dare you say that?" She tightened her hold and shook it.

She didn't want to think about her mother at the moment, but Mashaka left her no choice. Her mother was her father's second wife and, according to hushed whispers, a female vulture who preyed on married men. Karma gets you; they applauded when her mother got cheated by her father. Her mother hadn't seen that coming. They got divorced a year ago, and her father was still in a relationship with the third woman. The last time her parents were seen together was when Tara was in the hospital.

"You wicked thing!" Tara snarled.

Did I say something wrong?

Tara knew it was provoking her, but she couldn't help it.

She grabbed a knife from the knife holder and waved it above her left hand. "I will kill you," she warned, her voice bordering on hysteria.

A soft thud met her ears. Tara turned and was met with the bewildered, slack-jawed look of her domestic helper. On the floor were her clothes, which she had given for washing and dry cleaning.

Tara?

Tara looked back at Mashaka.

You know what they say about you, don't you, or shall I remind you?

9

BLISTER BEETLE AND A STORY

Those who are lonely yearn for connection.

While those in love suffer in it.

What is one supposed to do?

Sometimes I tell myself that I'm too old to write about love or keep a journal. I close the journal and shift my attention to the sound.

He jabbers on. Rarely shuts up. I wish he had a pause or mute button like the radio I once owned. Where is it now? The radio. Did I sell it to a scrap metal collector? Over the past few years my memory has gone a bit fuzzy and unreliable.

Humming to himself, he closely inspects something between his thumb and index finger. He then bounds over to me, halting two feet away, and brings his hand up closer to my eyes. Squinting, I lean my head down to make out the shape of a blister beetle with a black body displaying vibrant red spots.

My head snaps up. I aim for a shriek, but what escapes my lips sounds like the neigh of a horse.

"It's a blister beetle! Throw it away and go wash your hands thoroughly with soap," I instruct.

He doesn't move. He doesn't throw away that thing even though that thing looks dead. I have never been good with living beings that are slow to follow well-meaning instructions.

"I said throw it away." I invoke my past life's stern academic voice. I'm pretty sure my impatience with his reluctance is all over my face by now.

He does as I say, and after giving me a look that I cannot decipher, sprints into the house.

I never imagined I'd be in this situation that I'm in. Never thought I'd outlive my sister. Never thought I'd become in charge of my sister's great-grandchild at my current age.

The familiar song of the white-rumped shama from the neem tree in the garden does not comfort my aging soul.

……

His arrival affects my sleep. The momentous changes in his young life, however, don't seem to have made a dent on his sleep, as his inexhaustible energy throughout the day is the proof of that.

I toss my legs out of the bed and mewl at the shooting pain in my right knee. Another thing that has happened since his arrival is that people around me have begun to remind me of my age as if I have forgotten about it. I take a deep lungful of air, lift my right leg, and wiggle a bit. I feel no pain. I then pause and listen and hear no sound other than distant bird calls. I haul myself out of the bed and prepare for the day.

After breakfast, I spray water on the leaves of the indoor plants by the window — a snake plant, a silver satin pothos, a white and green striped spider plant, an oval-shaped Chinese evergreen, and a peace lily flashing a white bloom sitting snugly in their respective cream-coloured pots. These plants don't ask much. Sprinkle some water once in a while, and that's it. I move on to dust the bookshelves, which don't require dusting, but I do it anyway. And then I find my old radio tucked away in a cardboard box, wedged between two other boxes with forgotten items of bygone years that had been discarded in the storage room. At least, now I know I haven't given it to the scrap collector. When bending and moving my body invokes dormant pains in different parts of my body, I can't stop feeling envious looking at his young, vigorous body.

He's drawing something on paper while prattling on as usual. He keeps himself busy throughout the day, and I can't be happier. At noon, I watch him picking up a dry leaf from the garden. His mouth moves, and I wonder what is coming out of it. I dare not move from my porch chair. I wonder if he misses his parents. We haven't spoken about his parents yet. I'm not going to bring them up unless he does it first. My niece's refusal to take him in doesn't surprise me after she had cut ties with her daughter a decade ago for marrying a man of another nationality.

Life is full of surprises, and I hadn't seen this coming, not even in my dreams.

……

The air is cool after the rain. I enjoy such weather to contemplate life. But no calm lasts forever.

My ritual of sitting quietly on the veranda after dinner gets a rude shock when he asks me to tell him a story. He sits crossed-legged on the floor. His face unnerves me. He is looking at me eagerly, waiting. I rack my old brain and come out empty. I don't know any stories. Stories that would entertain him. Stories that would entertain any child. I could tell him the fascinating and not-so-fascinating details of different bugs and insects, or how every plant, animal and fungus play a crucial role in the survival of our ecosystem. The sort of stuff I taught a classroom of half bored and half curious students for more than thirty-five years before retiring twenty-eight years ago. But those things won't interest him. The type of stories he wishes to hear is not in my brain. So I try to conjure one.

"There was a man," I begin, and rest both my arms on the chair's armrest. "He went to a forest alone, which he shouldn't have, as he was told not to. I don't understand why some people have to be rebellious. So he went to the forest, and this forest was not your usual forest, okay? Have you heard the story of *Hansel and Gretel*?"

He nods. "Mom told me that story once."

What else did your mom tell you?

"Oh, great. So this story is just like that. There was something sinister in the forest just like the witch in *Hansel and Gretel*." I stop. That's it. I don't really know where I am planning to take the story next. Making children's stories shouldn't be this hard. I look out of the door at the orchid tree with vermillion flowers drooping from branches, the Cassia Javanica with its pink bloom, and, a short distance from them, a Kachnar tree without a bloom. Despite their visual beauty, they grant me no inspiration, so I tilt my head to the darkening sky. Sometimes waiting is just futile. Neither nature nor the sky comes to my rescue. I have never told children stories, and I realize in my first attempt I'm failing miserably.

"Do you know that beluga whales are called 'sea canaries'?"

"What is a beluga whale?" He asks.

I don't own a smartphone to show him what beluga whales look like.

"Never mind. Aren't you hungry?" I try to distract him.

As I fear, he shakes his head. "Fine. So, where was I? Oh, right, the man, the disobedient man. So he is in the forest, where he shouldn't be, and he notices something lurking behind some trees. Now he's regretting coming to the forest. But he doesn't back out. That is his mistake because he gets killed by this thing, whatever that thing is. So the moral of the story is never to disobey or be a rebel, as you can end up getting killed."

He stares at me, as if not believing that the story actually ended. I turn and gesture to the wall clock. "See the time. It's time for dinner." I haul myself out of the chair and totter to the kitchen, leaving him on the floor.

......

I don't know anything about his life before he came to live with me. His great-grandmother, my sister, died a decade before he was born; his maternal grandmother hasn't even seen or met him, and I don't know much about his grandparents on his father's side. Was I told they died or something? Maybe. I don't remember exactly, but I think someone did tell me something about some dead grandparents. Can't expect my old brain to keep track of all dead old people, can I?

I realize the house is quiet. I put my magazine down on the chunky, rustic wooden table, which has been in the house for over twenty-five years. As old as a grandchild, if I had one. Wasn't he watching TV? I try to remember. Why has the house fallen quiet all of a sudden? Well, the quietness was the norm till his arrival a month ago, but now it's an anomaly. My heart is torn. I really don't wish to leave the comfort of the thick padded armchair in my bedroom. I have noted that the snugness of its soft cushion makes it hard for me to get up. So much changed as the years rolled by. I remember the first year post-retirement, I was quite restless. I struggled to keep myself busy. But gradually I learned to embrace the moments of serenity in idleness.

I go against my poor heart and drag myself to the living room. The TV is off, and the living room is empty. I shuffle to the threshold of the front door and pause. I squint at the sun-drenched garden, and it takes me a few seconds to find him crouched near the pots of Jade mini and a snake plant. He is nudging the ground with his finger. He then lifts his other hand to his eyes. What is he doing, and what is he looking at? I wonder as fear mounts in me. Did he find another blister beetle? Oh, what am I going to do with this kid?

"What are you doing there?" I ask as I cross the threshold but stay on the porch.

He shoots up off the ground. His left hand clasping into a loose fist swings back as if shielding it from me.

I seriously cannot do this. If it's another blister beetle, and that too a live one, and it gives him rashes and welts, I'm not going to take him to a doctor or care for him.

Perhaps whatever he is hiding in his palm manages to crawl out of his not-so-tight fist and skitters to the ground, causing him to turn swiftly behind him. He leans down, I shout, and he stops. He slowly straightens up and looks at the ground, his eyes moving away from him. Whatever it is, I cannot see. Good eyesight didn't sustain me to my old age.

"I told you not to go around touching all those bugs and critters." I hope my voice sounds as displeased as I am.

He looks at me, then back to the ground at a distance. Then his head swings around swiftly, and his eyes assess every pot on the ground.

"Come inside and watch TV," I tell him.

"Not interested," he responds, his eyes turning back to the ground.

I leave him there and scamper to the comfort of my chair in the bedroom.

As night descends onto the land, I set the table and call him from wherever he is in the house. I don't have to wait much before he comes trotting to the table. My initial worry of him being mischievous or recalcitrant tapered off within the first three days.

We eat in silence, just the way I like, and which he has come to sense very early on. He's not a picky eater and eats everything I serve on his plate. Sometimes I notice the way he chews his food too many times suggesting he has had enough, yet continues to finish the food on his plate. After dinner, I assume my usual place in the front doorway, doing my usual thing of staring out into the quiet dark, peppered with the intermittent noise of humans and animals. A giggle to my right interjects the peace, and I turn to the sound. He sits cross legged on the sofa, watching TV. He doesn't ask me to tell him a story tonight, which isn't surprising considering how disastrous my first attempt was. I'm relieved but I also feel slightly miffed.

Cartoon characters' voices trickle out of the TV. When his great grandmother and I were of his age, we lived in a village where electricity was a luxury. The night was for the humans what it was for the animals. A time to surrender to slumber. But the artificial lights toppled that nature's rule for the humans, keeping them awake and alert as long as they desired. I won't lie, there is something beautiful about the otherwise dark land illuminating at night. It brings to mind some of the ways nature alights the dark landscape, like the bioluminescent mushrooms growing on dead bamboo sticks in the West hills district in Meghalaya, and the zillions of fireflies coming out in the open after sunset during the months of May and June in Purushwadi forest in Maharashtra.

……

I call a plumber to fix the leak in the kitchen sink. I couldn't prepare the breakfast I was planning to because of the leak. While I wait for the plumber in the dining room, I hear a faint pattering of running footsteps above me. When did he go to the terrace?

I seriously don't want to think about the coming days. I don't want the summer to end. I don't want to think about the schools he'll have to enroll in. Grant me a never-ending summer.

An hour later the plumber is done fixing the leak. The plumber looks at him, standing near me. Five minutes ago, he emerged from somewhere, having spent half of his energy.

"I heard he's your great-grandson," the plumber says, with a smile crinkling his eyes.

"My late sister's great-grandson," I correct him. He shrugs as if it makes no difference, then turns to glance at the sink and walks out.

At noon, I find him trying to read the titles of the books on the shelf in the study room. After running his eyes over the books at his eye level, his head slowly tilts up. I don't have any books suitable for his age. I don't even know if he likes to read or not. Did his parents read him bedtime stories? What was the ritual before going to bed? What was his life like? I will never know.

When night cloaks the land, I perch on my usual spot by the front door, and fix my eyes outdoors. Rustling leaves accompany my heartbeats. I don't know how much time passes, but suddenly I realize I cannot hear the sound of TV. I turn to the room. At one moment, he's on the sofa, looking bored, and twisting his lips at weird angles, and the next he's marching towards me. I brace myself.

"Can you tell me a story?" He asks, slightly swaying his body side to side. I look away briefly, then nod my head, and he sits cross-legged on the floor.

"There was a man. Not the one in the previous story. That man is gone. This man also goes to the forest to cut some wood. After cutting some wood, he prepares to go back home, but, alas, he realizes that he's lost. He doesn't know how to return home. And it's getting dark." I pause and look at him. His eyes are fixed on the undercut of the front door, his lips slightly apart with a serious expression on his young face. Probably he's imagining the man's unpleasant situation.

I carry on, hoping fervently that this story doesn't meet the disastrous and disappointing end the previous one did.

"He doesn't know how to get out of the dark jungle."

"He doesn't?" He lifts his eyes to mine, with the solemn expression intact on his face.

"No, he doesn't. With no light to guide him, he just walks randomly, hoping he somehow manages to make it out of the forest. Then, he sees a light in the distance. He follows the light and finds a house. This house was brightly lit. He hesitates briefly before knocking on the door. After a few seconds, the door opens, and there stands an old woman."

"Like you?"

"Yes, like me. Seeing him, the old woman begins to smile from ear to ear. The poor man is too scared at this point. It so happens that he has also heard the story of Hansel and Gretel, so he's wary of the old woman. The old woman invites the man in. The man has no choice but to take her offer. Upon entering, he notices that the house is not that different from other houses except that it is unusually bright. The man tells the old woman his plight, and the woman nods her head with her smile never leaving her face. The old woman tells him that he can sleep at her house for the night and can leave in the morning. Again the man has no choice but to accept her offer. Even though he is safe in the house and not out in a dark forest, he finds it hard to relax, you know. The old woman leaves him in the living room and vanishes within the house. Shortly, he begins to hear the voices of two people.

"Who is the other person?" He asks.

"A boy. And this boy comes out to the living room and cheerfully introduces himself. The man tells the boy why he's there, and the boy tells the man he'll take him safely out of the jungle and back to his home. At this point, the old woman comes out and is not happy to hear that. She insists that the man stay there for the night, but the boy insists on helping him. The man is not sure what is going on as he watches the old woman and the boy arguing. In the end the boy leads the man to his home."

"Why not stay at the old woman's house for the night?" He asks.

"What do you think?" I ask.

"She was going to eat him. The boy saved the man," he says more to himself.

A lull follows. Maybe I'm not a bad storyteller.

10

RAIN-SOAKED HEART

Tall and gangly, he is staring at the bare walls with a paint spray bottle in his hand.

I try to kick-start my scooter over and over again. In the passion and fury, I stub my toe, and my jaw tightens.

I should have known better. In my experience, once my scooter decides to stop unexpectedly, no amount of making it start again works.

There are few onlookers. I know help won't be that far. I look at him, hoping.

Hoping. Hoping.

My hope dies abruptly. A wiry young boy of about 20 years struts towards me confidently and gestures to me to step aside while he performs his magic on my stubborn scooter.

I look at the tall and gangly. His back is turned to me, as always. Turned to the world as he spray-painted our drab city walls, which, for some reason, city authorities do not wish to see adorned.

I have seen him having heated arguments with cops. I have seen him in different locations, staring mutely at the bare walls, as if invoking the deity of creativity. I have seen him shaking his paint spray vigorously before transforming the ugly walls.

It always surprises me when I watch him. Because it seems I'm the only one noticing him. People pass by him without sparing him a glance. Yes, except for the cops who give him a hard time whenever they see him unleashing his artwork.

A familiar sound turns my eyes to where it should have been. The scooter has come to life. I thank the young man and perch on my vehicle. I don't spare the 'tall and gangly' another look and speed off to my destination.

......

It starts pouring by the time I climb the front porch steps. A flash of lightning sizzles the sky, accompanied by its companion thunder. A grey sky upsets me. I wish I could keep the sky always bright and sunny.

I shuffle through the door, and there she is, staring out of the window with the TV on and seeking her attention. The dismal weather has quickly sucked the last ounce of natural light from the living room, leaving it dark and gloomy.

"Maa."

She turns her head. A brief look of puzzlement crosses over her eyes but soon passes away. I wish the gray clouds coating the sky would pass away too.

"Did you eat your lunch?" I ask, hoping she answers in the affirmative. She has been skipping her meals lately, reasoning that she didn't feel hungry. The problem is she has completely lost her appetite and is never hungry.

"Yes."

I try to read her face. Did she sound unsure? Could she be lying or have forgotten about whether she has eaten lunch or not?

I move closer to her. "Are you sure? What are you watching here?" I turn to the TV.

She follows my eyes, and immediately confusion creates frown lines on her forehead. "I don't—

I don't let her finish. "Well, it looks like some reality show."

She doesn't say anything, simply stares at the TV. "I'll freshen up," I say and head to my bedroom.

The rain battering the rooftop should have quelled my negative emotions, but it doesn't. There was a time when it used to. There was a time I used to enjoy rain. Rain meant familiarity. Rain meant comfort. Rain meant certainty.

But now, it makes my heart heavier, as if all the raindrops falling to the ground are collecting in my chest.

The crackle of thunder echoes through the sky.

I shutter the window and turn on the light as everything on land mirrors the grayness above.

I wish I could spray paint the sky bright and baby blue now.

……

I brake abruptly. Immediately someone honks from behind, and a man on a motorbike gives me a very dirty look before speeding off. To my left, the bare gray wall of yesterday is sporting a new look. There are two children on it. A young boy on a cycle pedaling furiously to catch up with a young girl a few meters ahead of him. The girl's neck is slightly twisted sideways as if she is trying to look at the boy behind her.

I sigh. Is the boy ever going to catch up with the girl? Is the girl ever going to manage to see the boy's face? Are they related? Friends? Only half of the children's faces are visible to the viewers, and yet the girl's smirk is undeniable. Could it be because she knows he'd never catch up with her, no matter how hard he tries?

I check my wristwatch. I accelerate my scooter lest I get late for work.

……

I chug water from my water bottle and screw the cap back on. I don't feel hungry, and it doesn't always happen. In fact, an insatiable appetite is the only constant thing in my life. The colleague who invited everyone in the morning to her marriage the coming Saturday is talking animatedly with another at the coffee machine. She has been smiling for hours now. She didn't even eat her lunch, did she? I have read somewhere that some people lose their appetite when they're extremely happy.

I eye the remaining food in my lunch box before closing it shut.

......

I cannot believe my eyes.

I had just stepped out of the chemist shop, and there he was, across the road, shaking his paint spray can, ready to attack the walls before him.

Someone bumps into my shoulder, and I suddenly realize I have stopped in my tracks. I stuff the plastic bag with my mother's medication into my handbag and take a few steps forward.

Something else catches my eye, and I smile wide. A small boy crouched on the pavement is watching the tall and gangly. At least now I know someone is as intrigued by the artist as me.

My heart skips a beat seeing a cop on a motorbike slowing down with his head turned towards the tall and gangly. Relief washes over me when the cop speeds off.

Still as a statue, he's gazing at the wall. Is he not sure what he wants to paint? Or having another pair of eyes—curious eyes—making him nervous? How would he react if he knew there is another pair of eyes that has seen him work four times?

I take my phone out of my handbag, pretending to call someone, and press the phone to my ears while my eyes sweep over him. It is ridiculous. No one is watching him or me. Why not observe him work as unabashedly and carefree as the child with his small, wiry arms wrapped around his bent knees?

We both watch. The little boy and me. From near and from across the road. That is my way. I never get closer. Bodies move around me as I watch formless colors coalesce into a story on the wall. A woman with a handbag swinging slightly behind her, the tip of which is clutched by a little girl following her. Two blue and black birds fly overhead.

The man freezes again, his hand holding the spray can limp at his side. The boy below doesn't move either.

A low rumble shifts my attention skyward. Heaven has begun to darken. Time for me to head home.

......

She is pacing the room when I enter.

She stumbles towards me. "I forgot something, and I cannot find it." She sounds just as confused.

I slide my handbag onto a chair. "Okay. Do you remember what it is?" I ask her gently.

Her hair is wet; some strands have clumped together and are lying flat against her scalp. She holds my eyes only briefly before they fly all over the wall behind me.

"No. No. I don't remember. That's the problem. I don't remember what it is."

......

I don't allow her to enter the kitchen, and she is not happy about it. I can hear her grumbling in the dining room. Surprisingly, she doesn't disobey me and enter the kitchen anyway. What can be the reason? It bothers me.

I set the table. She's quiet. Very quiet. Something that's becoming her second skin. I sit across from her and wait for her to serve her food, but she doesn't.

"Maa?" I call for her attention. She looks up at me, and I gesture to her plate. She lowers her eyes to her plate and slowly begins to fill it with food. I cannot keep the displeasure from clouding my face seeing the small portion on her plate.

"Maa, you're not a child. Is this how much you're going to eat tonight?" I ask.

She stirs the food on her plate with a spoon but doesn't look as if she wants to eat it. She doesn't say her usual "*I'm not hungry*" as she has already used it as an excuse numerous times. I watch her stir her rice a few more times and then reluctantly bring it to her mouth.

As I eat my food, my thoughts skitter to the artist. I haven't seen him for a week now. I always pass by one of his artworks on my way to or from work. Seeing his artwork always makes me wonder—Is it his calling? Is he sure about it? How exactly does it feel to do something that one's passionate about? To be honest, I don't even know what I'm passionate about. In fact, I don't delve deep into it, perhaps to keep the truth of finding out that I am not passionate about anything.

With good grades in school and college came the decision to get a career that'd pay well. That's what my parents did, and as their daughter, I was expected to do. Never once did I stop to think if that's what I truly wanted to do.

Never did either of my parents try to evaluate what I am good at. What a waste of thinking about it now! It's the fault of the 'tall and gangly.' Seeing him engrossed in his artwork has made me question my non-existing passion and career choice.

For me, my career is just my career. I don't derive any sort of pleasure from my work. The idea of truly enjoying one's work never crossed my mind. Until I saw him.

"Did you find what you were looking for?" I ask.

She stops eating abruptly. When her eyes meet mine, confusion and annoyance struggle to take the upper hand.

"No, I didn't," she says.

I gesture to her to continue eating. "It's fine. Maybe you'll find it tomorrow."

A moment of hesitation later, she continues to eat.

I refill my plate with three ladles of rice. Tonight my appetite is in full swing.

I look at her. Distant, confused, sorrowful. These have become her current face.

"Maa, did you like the book I bought you?"

Again the look of confusion mars her face. Then the realization emerges like cicadas erupting from the ground.

"No, no, I didn't," she says, shaking her head of gray, shoulder-length hair which was as black as a raven once. Her eyes look tired, I note. Isn't she sleeping well at night?

"Why is that?"

"I couldn't follow the plot," she says, chewing her food slowly.

……

I'm hungry. I'm thirsty. And I'm annoyed with myself. Why on earth am I even doing this? I have been riding around to different parts of the town for an hour now.

Where is he?

Night is descending, and I better be heading home, I remind myself for the fifth time.

……

She has been making up stories that never happened.

Sometimes I hear her talking to an empty room as if having a conversation with someone.

The rainy season has arrived, and I hate the endlessly gray August days.

But there was a time when the wet, dull August days didn't bother me at all. There was always a time that was very different from now.

A distant rumble. Standing by the edge of the bed, I wait.

The sound of rain pulls me to the window. Rain pelts the coconut trees that fringe our house. Rain drenches everything outside. It also soaks my mood. A wave of lethargy washes over me.

A loud bang of a window somewhere from the house. Then another.

"What is this sound? Where is it coming from?" I hear her wonder aloud.

I turn and walk through the hallway to the dining room, where she is closing the windows.

"Did you hear that? These windows were banging so loud," she says, turning to me with a worried expression.

Loud noises have become intolerable to her.

"Why is it raining so hard?" She laments, looking mournfully at the closed window.

"It's quite natural for this month," I remind her.

She turns to meet my eyes. "You won't believe me, but my parents' house had a tin roof, and I used to greatly enjoy the sound of rain falling on it." She shakes her head in disbelief. "I cannot imagine falling asleep to that noise anymore."

"Things change," I tell her.

She doesn't say anything. Creases of puzzlement appear on her forehead. Then just as quickly, it disappears with another look of realization.

"Oh, the food is on the stove. It's probably cooked," she hurries past me to the kitchen.

"What are you making?" I ask. She doesn't respond.

……

My stomach growls, and I ignore it. No amount of food satisfies it, so I have stopped serving its demands. When it is time for me to feed it, I feed it; after that, I pay no heed to its whining.

A group of college boys are watching him from a distance. Some are laughing and bantering while watching him. Others watch him quietly.

I have been looking for him for over a month now. Why has he suddenly appeared today? Could he have come out of his cocoon because of the clear, blue sky?

But the weather is no inspiration to him. The clouds he's creating are dark and ominous. Before our eyes, the menacing clouds on the wall burst open, and the raindrops pelt on the hapless three men with downcast eyes, seemingly rushing, holding a blue plastic cover over their heads.

Will they ever make it to the nearby shelter?

……

The house illuminates with all the lights on.

She's sitting in the porch chair, looking tense and distraught. I park my scooty and close the gate. Her eyes never leave mine as I ascend the porch stairs.

"I don't know what it is, but I know I forgot something important," she says, with a pained expression.

"I know, Maa. I know."

11

SHALL BREATHE NOW

Cooking in the humid, sultry weather was pure torture. Mikhila turned on the exhaust fan and waited; a pearl of sweat hung from the tip of her nose precariously. Another slithered through the side of her face. Without warning, the salty drop of sweat dropped in her coffee mug in front of her. She closed her eyes and felt the heat pressing in from all sides. Her landline rang in the living room. Mikhila didn't move, and the ringing died down.

She peered over the windows shadowed by the curtains and struggled with the idea of opening them and airing the room. She stepped back as steam rose from the saucepan of oats. Mikhila was suddenly irritated and wondered why she continued to eat oats for breakfast; she never liked it in the first place. Like most others, she preferred to eat Indian food for breakfast, which was anything but sweet.

"Mikhi, look at the amount of oil that goes into making most Indian food!" Tanveer had grimaced at the *parantha* she made the day after their marriage.

"Consuming excess oil on a daily basis can harm your body. Let's decide one thing. We'll eat oats for breakfast daily, and we can have Indian meals for lunch and dinner," he said.

Mikhila's face and voice couldn't contain her displeasure. "Daily? Oats?"

Tanveer squinted, lips pursed. "Fine. On weekends we'll have whatever you want to eat for breakfast. Come on now, give me that smile I fell for."

Tanveer!

Mikhila's eyes darted towards the draped windows. If she opened the window and saw the bright sun and people moving around in their perfect world, a part of her might yearn for all of it, and that would be a betrayal to her mourning, she chided herself. Sighing, she turned off the heat. Grabbing her mug, she walked to the living room and sat on the couch.

"I am lucky anyway that I do not have to be outside in this sweltering heat. I could die of sunstroke." Mikhila muttered, surprising herself.

It was the first time she heard her voice in the last six days. Thirty-seven days had passed since the death of her husband. Thirty-seven days since he was lost to the sea. Thirty-seven days since she last saw him or his body. For four days she waited eagerly for the call to inform her that Tanveer's body was recovered or, that he was somehow alive, by a miracle. But after a month, her hope turned to despair, and she shut herself in their house, refusing to attend any calls. By then she dreaded the idea of identifying his body or what was left of him. To see him and yet not to see the face she loved dearly would kill her. She lost her sleep and would wake up screaming in the middle of the night. She would dream of the police knocking on her door and dragging her to a morgue to identify her husband. She would always wiggle out of their hands and scream to let her go because she knew her husband was just a stinking, swollen mass of flesh now. The recurring nightmare made her dread sleep altogether.

Mikhila sipped her coffee reluctantly and breathed in the musty smell hanging over the house. Setting the mug on the glass table, she closed her eyes and imagined how her life would have turned out if she had had a child. Unlike some women who always dreamed of motherhood, she had never considered it, not until the third year of their marriage. That's when she noticed the subtle changes in his attitude towards her. Tanveer never wanted a child, but Mikhila had hoped that he would change eventually. Even the sound of children playing in the neighbourhood annoyed and irritated him. As the year passed by, she lost all hope and even became weary of bringing up the topic of having a child.

Mikhila began to sob when she opened her eyes.

"If only I had a child, I wouldn't have felt so lonely."

……

Navigating in the dark by touching the familiar objects around her, Mikhila switched on the bathroom light and entered inside. The woman looking back at her in the mirror was a mess.

She had pale skin, sunken cheeks, two dark pouches under the eyes, unkempt hair, and a heart desolated by the loss.

Mikhila tugged at the loose, dry, chapped skin on her lips, drawing a bead of blood. She turned the faucet and splashed water over her mouth. She sucked at her bottom lip and felt slightly nauseous at the metallic taste of blood.

Mikhila was startled when the silence of the house was once again broken by the vexatious, familiar sound of the landline ringing.

Her stomach rumbled, and she ambled towards the kitchen and switched on the light. Though she knew she wouldn't find anything edible in it, she opened the refrigerator and peered at the empty shelves. Groaning, she closed the refrigerator door. Looking over her kitchen cabinets, she suddenly felt tired and rejected the idea of cooking.

As she was about to turn off the light, she noticed, to her delight, the saucepan with the untouched oats. Grabbing a spoon, she gobbled up the cold oats and found them tasty for the first time. Just as she swallowed the last of it, the ringing started again. A tear fell from her eye, and she started trembling.

"It's time you faced the truth." She choked on her words.

She felt as if her feet would give away, but she managed to walk to the living room without bumping into anything and lifted the receiver with her sweaty palm.

"Hello?" The woman on the other side sounded breathless.

Mikhila didn't respond.

"At last! You picked!" The voice on the other side exclaimed, and then, unsure if Mikhila was still on the line, she repeated, "Hello? Hello?"

"Who is this?" Mikhila asked, bracing for the worst.

"Ha," the woman laughed, "Mikhila? Mikhila, it's you, right?"

Mikhila wanted to answer in the negative, "Hmmm."

"I have been trying to reach you for almost a week."

"Who is this?" Mikhila was confused now.

The woman didn't reply right away and then said, "If I tell you who I am, you won't hang up, will you?"

Mikhila didn't feel right about the whole conversation. She shook her head, reluctantly.

"Veena."

"Who?"

"You don't remember me? Me? Right, well, it's been almost six years now. How time flies! You seriously don't remember me? I'm Tanveer's—"

Mikhila slammed the receiver down and, on second thoughts, replaced it on the table. Her breathing became faster, and finding the couch, she slumped on it and buried her face in her palms. Despite the humidity, a chill ran down her spine, and she struggled to calm her breathing.

"You are the last person I want to remember," Mikhila muttered inside her cupped palms.

......

Bleary-eyed, Mikhila went through all the stuff of Tanveer to distract herself from the phone call two days ago. Sleep had been elusive since Tanveer's death, but she couldn't sleep a wink the past two days. Her head was drumming, and she had been feeling nauseous since morning.

She opened Tanveer's wardrobe and felt some of his shirts and t-shirts. She took out a burgundy shirt, his favourite, and holding it tightly to her chest, she cried. She wished to feel Tanveer against her. She wanted his arms around her. *But that can never happen.*

Later, Mikhila made coffee and drank it in Tanveer's coffee mug. She sauntered through her memory lane as she sipped, remembering the first time they had met.

Mikhila, a dental receptionist, was twenty-nine when she first met Tanveer Katri. Before meeting him, she was a woman determined to remain single for the rest of her life. She firmly believed that one could only be happy by remaining unmarried and experiencing the beauty of life alone. Her parents got divorced when she was thirteen. She lived with her mother until she turned nineteen, around the time her mother remarried. Neither of her parents kept in touch with her, and as the years passed, she estranged herself from them.

On a chilly, late November morning, Tanveer asked her to get the dentist's appointment. He had to wait for thirty-five minutes for his turn to come. Since he was the only one in the waiting room, he struck up a conversation with Mikhila, asking her about her life and family. Even though Mikhila didn't ask him anything in return, he told her about himself. He was a thirty-eight years old financial advisor, married to a travel agent, had no children, and was living a very comfortable and happy life except for the bothersome toothache. After he was checked by the dentist, before leaving, he stopped in front of her desk and asked her if she could have coffee with him someday. Impulsively, Mikhila nodded. It didn't take them long to go out more often.

Whenever she was with Tanveer, Mikhila always knew that her actions were wrong and she was voluntarily causing discord in a couple's marriage.

After around nine months of dating, Tanveer proposed to her one day. Her suppressed guilt unveiled itself, all at once. Mikhila refused to meet him for a whole week. Not only was she whacked with guilt, but staying away from Tanveer hurt her even more. On his insistence, she agreed to meet him one day, relieved secretly. He convinced her that he never loved his wife as much as he loved her. He was filing for a divorce, and it was good for all three of them.

......

Mikhila sat cross-legged on her bed. She glanced up at the wall clock. The bedroom walls were mostly adorned with her and

Tanveer's photographs. That was one of the things he loved—taking their photos. Whenever they travelled, he would request a passerby to take their photos. Mikhila's gaze travelled from one photo to another till it stopped on one.

It was her favourite. Tanveer's too.

In the photo, Tanveer was cupping her face with his lips touching her forehead. Mikhila's arms were draped over his neck. Groves of coconut trees lined the backgrounds. Though their faces weren't visible, it was undoubtedly their most beautiful photo together. The photo was taken at Palolem Beach in Goa. Though widely promoted for its dolphin-spotting tours, Mikhila and Tanveer did not spot a single dolphin during their stay.

Mikhila heard the sound she dreaded. And yet, she sprinted towards it, and this time the receiver was lifted on the fourth ring.

"Hello?"

"What do you want?"

"See, I knew you'd hang up the moment I told you who I am, but…"

"Vee..." Mikhila could not even bring herself to utter the name. "Veena, why are you calling? And how did you get this number?"

Mikhila shut her eyes as a chuckle met her ear, "From your husband. My ex."

Mikhila thought she didn't hear it right. "What? Tanveer?"

"I know it might enrage you, but he..."

"That's not possible! You are lying!"

"Sure. You are entitled to think whatever you want, but Tanveer called me about eight or nine months ago, crying..."

"You are lying," Mikhila whispered, her hand shaking in disbelief.

"No. He was crying about a lot of things, including his dreary and monotonous life. How he wished to escape from it, and if only he could press the right button on the remote to change his life and transport him to another world, he would have done that. I have no idea what 'remote' he was blabbering about. Like I mentioned, the first time he called me was around nine months ago. He called me from the number I remember. I didn't bother to answer it. Two days after that I got a call from an unknown number, and it happened to be him. The moment I realised it was him, I disconnected the call. Just a few weeks after the second call, I got a call from another unknown number. It was him. But before I could disconnect, I heard him crying. That's when he started complaining about his life. The last time he called me was from your landline number. He didn't say much. Simply apologized for calling me thrice before and hung up on me."

Mikhila drew the receiver away from her and held it against her hip as tears spilled from her eyes. She really wanted to break the phone, go to the comfort of her bed, and sleep away from this nightmare. Instead, she wiped her eyes with her other hand and brought the receiver to her ear.

"Hello? Hello? Mikhila? Are you there?"

"Mmm."

"Are you okay?" asked Veena.

Mikhila knew Veena was not a bit concerned. In fact, if she closed her eyes, she could see Veena grinning.

I can't blame her, thought Mikhila.

"Why?" Mikhila wondered aloud.

"Why did he call? For one, he sounded drunk as a skunk, and second, he's a rascal."

Mikhila winced. "Don't. He's…"

"He loses interest in his women as fast as people lose interest in their clothes."

"He passed away."

The silence on the other side was profound. So much so that a tiny part of her thought the whole phone call was a fabrication of her imagination.

"I know. A friend of mine told me."

Mikhila suddenly felt weary but felt companionship in Veena. There was no reason to, but she felt she needed to tell her everything.

"I see. So, he left a suicide note on the dresser, and by the time you returned from the market, he was gone with what seemed like an intention to end his life by drowning. How convenient! Do you concur with all this?" Veena said.

"Please..."

"You didn't find his body," Veena stated. "They didn't, I mean, right?"

"No."

"You will not find his body anytime soon, at least not until he actually decides to end his life."

Mikhila was perplexed. But at the same time she didn't want to know what Veena had meant. *I should hang up before it's too late*, thought Mikhila.

Stop it. Stop it. Stop it.

Despite her mind cautioning her, Mikhila asked the question that had been nagging her since the revelation, "Veena, could you give me the numbers he called you from?"

"Gladly. Just a second." In the brief silence that ensued, Mikhila heard a child's shriek followed by a giggle in the background. She wondered if Veena remarried and had a child. Instantly, the pain of being childless tugged at her heart. Veena's voice came over, and she read the numbers.

"The first two of them are his number. The last one is not," Mikhila said.

"Well, it is his. He hid the number from you. And I know why," Veena said.

Mikhila felt sick; her hands were clammy, and beads of perspiration formed on her forehead. She held the headrest of the couch tightly.

I must lie down, she thought.

"A week after I heard whispers of his suicide, for no reason, I dialed those three numbers. Two were switched off, the ones you said were his. The last one was answered by a woman. For a few seconds I was too surprised to speak. I didn't expect it to be answered at all. When I asked for Tanveer, the woman hung up on me. After that I tried twice, with the same result. The number was switched off. And probably discarded immediately."

Mikhila slammed the receiver down. Heaving, she tore the extension out of its socket and hurled the landline across the room.

She crumpled on the floor and wailed.

……

The air was slowly warming up with the ascending October sun. Mikhila placed the empty coffee cup on the table and touched the bell sleeves of her mustard top. She leaned back on the porch chair, her eyes on her moss green palazzo. She'd never worn them out, not even once. She was going to change that.

She was suddenly angry with herself. She was stupid, wasn't she? Buying something she liked but then not wearing it because her husband hated the colours. Upon seeing them, Tanveer even managed to look like a betrayed husband whose wife was caught cheating red-handed. So she dismissed them to the lower shelf of the wardrobe and forgot about their existence for many years.

Something moved in her periphery, drawing her gaze to the garden area by the gate where a yellow butterfly flitted above the foliage.

A wave of joy washed over her.

Behind her the house breathed in fresh air through its several open windows.

12

OMAN, THE DOLL

The strap of the flip-flop came off. He lifted his head and met his mother's glaring eyes. He knew it was not his fault, but under his mother's disapproving gaze, he felt guilty. He had a pair of shoes in the suitcase, but knowing his mother well, he didn't expect her to open the suitcase in the crowded railway station.

Nakul watched his mother's face contort in frustration. Or perhaps contempt. He wanted to kick the broken flip-flop into the reeking railway track, to forget about its existence. But his mother wouldn't like that.

Someone bumped into his shoulder, and the memory of his past flickered out. A wizened old man in a brown tweed coat apologized and walked by. Nakul turned his gaze on a woman and a small boy on a bench. He knew they were mother and son as they were seated in the adjoining compartment in the train. A broken sandal dangled from the boy's hand, which he swung playfully back and forth. Commuters and travelers rushed past Nakul to get to their respective destinations. Nakul was not in a hurry. He stalled. He wheeled his luggage to the nearby bench and pressed his phone to his ear, pretending to be on a call. Then he sneaked a glance at the mother-son duo. The mother opened a small suitcase and pulled out a plastic bag. Her hand went inside the plastic and came out carrying a small green flip-flop. With a smile, she placed it in front of her son's feet. Nakul looked away immediately. He rose to his feet and hurried out of the railway station as fast as he could.

He didn't want the drive home to end. He wanted to tell the driver to drive as slowly as he could. Nakul wiped his clammy hands on his jeans for the third time as he stared out of the car window. He tried to relax by taking long, slow, deep breaths. But when he remembered that his mother had told him to do this whenever he became excessively worried before exams, he immediately stopped. He avoided looking at the rear view mirror, where the driver kept stealing glances at him.

When the familiar street arrived, Nakul almost jumped out of the car and ran away. He was disgusted with his timid heart ramming feverishly against his chest.

She was standing inside the gate. When the taxi stopped, he handed the fare to the driver and, to delay looking at his mother, watched the taxi drive away.

She opened the gate and asked, "How was the journey?"

He forced a small smile and turned to her. Nakul hoped his fake smile was enough to convey the message that his journey was fine. It worked. She gave a nod, and just then, a white, medium-sized dog came bounding out of the front door.

"Marcy, stop!" His mother commanded in a tone that echoed from his distant past. Something about the intonation made his heartbeat race. The dog, now two feet away from Nakul, curiously studied him with a wagging tail.

"Come," his mother said, turning her back.

......

The world was golden orange behind his closed eyelids. He stood at the window, relishing the warmth of the morning sun on his face. The house was deliciously quiet. Then, it wasn't. The barks of Marcy made his eyes open. He turned to his door. It was locked. A sniffing sound emerged from the undercut of his shut door; shortly thereafter, his mother gave a command in a gentle tone.

Nakul shifted his back to the window to look at the tall, narrow bookshelf cabinet. On the second shelf sat a rag doll. Nakul tried to recall its name in the dead of the night. After racking his brain, just as he felt himself drifting off, a word suddenly flashed in his mind's eye—Oman. But he couldn't recall why he named it that. Nakul turned to his phone for help. He searched the internet and found the meaning of the word. Oman meant,'a friend, protector, helper.' Right away, he was ferried to his past.

While chatting about the very unique name of a new transfer student, he and his classmates ended up sharing the meanings of their personal names. One scrawny boy, Oman, explained the meaning of his name. Nakul instantly liked the boy even though they weren't friends.

If his memory was to be trusted, Nakul loved that doll, and it made sense why the young Nakul would have named it Oman. The young Nakul needed someone for comfort. Then, life had gotten in the way of their once special bond. He was sent to boarding school and after returning, he had forgotten about it completely. The thing was, it wasn't even in his room all these years.

A tap on the door contorted his face into a grimace. Unwillingly, he stepped back from the window and proceeded to open the door. His mother looked intently at him, perhaps expecting him to say something, but Nakul remained mum.

"Your breakfast and tea are ready. Come, eat it hot," she said.

Once at the dining table, Nakul hoped fervently that his mother wouldn't eat with him. He noisily sipped his scalding hot tea as fast as his mouth could manage. He thought of taking his phone from his room to occupy himself but decided against it. Mercifully, the dining room window offered him a view of the back garden.

A four-foot-tall lemon tree and its taller companion, a pomegranate tree, looked neatly pruned. They reminded Nakul of schoolboys with freshly trimmed hair. Close by were sword-like snake plants standing poised beside two large pots of green chili plants. The slender tapioca trees lining the compound walls held his gaze with a tilt.

A hand appeared in his periphery. His mother set down a plate and a bowl before him. *Puri* and *mung bean curry*. His heart sank when she pulled a chair next to him and sank into it.

Marcy came padding towards them and cautiously edged closer to him. Nakul drew back his feet.

"Marcy, no! Don't disturb. You had your breakfast, girl," his mother said, in her matter-of-fact voice.

Marcy obeyed, somewhat reluctantly, and curled next to his mother's feet.

"So, what are your plans now that you have completed your studies?" His mother asked.

Nakul hated it. Talking about future plans. He hated it because he was unsure about it. Not exactly. He kind of knew what he was going to do but wasn't sure if that's what he actually wanted to do. He didn't want to rush into things. But he knew he didn't have much of a choice while he lived with his mother.

He cast a quick glance at his mother. "Eh, there's a doll in my room," he said.

She looked impassively at him. "It's yours. Don't you remember it?"

To avoid meeting her eyes, Nakul focused his attention on the glass of water before him. "Yeah. I just don't remember seeing it all these years. I mean, whenever I was home."

"I was cleaning the storeroom a few weeks ago when I found it there. I thought I'd put it back in your room."

Nakul didn't say anything and continued to eat his breakfast. A minute passed in peaceful silence.

"So, what have you planned to do next?"

It irked him. He hated her matter-of-fact voice and her 'practical-and-not emotional' approach to life. It had only been a day since he was home. Why did she have to bring up his 'future plans' on the first day'?

Nakul stuffed the last large piece of *puri* into his mouth and sprang to his feet. As he strenuously pushed the chewed food down his throat, he said, "I'll let you know soon."

Then he hurried back to his room.

……

Nakul inspected the rag doll. Other than looking a bit ratty, the doll looked fine. Its denim overalls, white shirt, and brown cap had no tear. Had he been careful with it as a child? The doll had clearly been a great deal of comfort to him as a child. As much as he remembered, he carried it with him at home, despite his mother's usual displeasure. He lifted a black curl of the doll and rubbed it between his thumb and index finger. He smiled at the similarity in their hair type.

That night he dreamed about his younger self. His younger self playing with his neighborhood friends. His younger self soaring in the sky like a bird and then suddenly crashing down to the Earth. His younger self dancing. His younger self getting scolded by his teachers and parents. His younger self cuddling his rag doll, and the rag doll whispering back an assurance, *Don't worry, Nakul. I'm here for you.*

Nakul woke up with a jolt. Swiftly he looked at the door. He thought he heard his bedroom door being pushed open, but it was clearly closed. Was it his dream? He then recalled his dream, and his head snapped towards the bookshelf. The rag doll was where he had left it last evening. Nakul laughed at the silliness of his fear.

Two days rolled by without much happening. Nakul stayed in his room, mostly painting and staring at the ceiling. His mother had gone to a distant relative's house, who was discharged from the hospital after gallbladder removal surgery. She had asked him to accompany her, but he had refused. She didn't insist.

The tranquility of the home was abruptly interrupted by the sound of his mother's voice. Nakul turned off the heat. Moments later, he padded into the living room, carrying his cup of black coffee. His mother entered the house, talking over the phone and clutching a paper bag. Without acknowledging him, she moved past him to the dining room and placed the paper bag on the table. Still on the call, she then proceeded to her room. Nakul returned to the dining room. He tore the paper bag, dug out a sweet bun from it, and went back to his room.

......

Nakul was not happy.

"Are you ready?" His mother asked from behind his bedroom door.

He ground his teeth in frustration. No, he wasn't ready. He was never ready to be in her company.

Nakul's head jerked to the bookshelf, imagining he heard a noise. The small curve of a smile on Oman's face appeared mischievous to Nakul's eyes.

Despite his plight, Nakul smiled. He moved towards the rag doll and muttered, "Are you taking delight in my condition?"

"Nakul?" His mother's voice had an edge to it, and Nakul knew it was time for him to face her.

He walked across the room and opened the door.

He could see his mother trying hard to conceal her displeasure at his tardiness. He answered her unsaid question before her penetrating gaze could unnerve him.

"I was in the bathroom."

A slight nod, and then, "Let's go then."

Twenty minutes later, they were in one of the busiest markets in their town. Nakul hadn't bothered to ask what they were there for or planning to buy. He didn't care. In the morning, while having another uncomfortable breakfast together, she simply told him that they'd leave for the market in an hour. She didn't ask him; she made her decision. He had no choice.

Walking by a lightning store, Nakul's eyes were briefly drawn to the glittering, luxurious chandeliers suspended from its ceiling. They moved past garment shops, electronic and footwear stores, and trinket and souvenir shops. It had been a year since he was in the market, and nothing had changed. Everything looked the same. Tendrils of vexation crept into him. Something should have changed, Nakul thought. But as soon as the thought occurred to him, he wasn't sure what he meant by that. What changes was he really implying? He cast a sideways glance at his mother, who looked poised and impassive. He shifted his gaze to the street vendors to quell the bubbling frustration.

"Do you want to buy something?" His mother looked at him.

Nakul simply shook his head.

"Okay. Let's just stop here for a moment." She had halted in front of a stall selling socks, handkerchiefs, and stoles.

Nakul stifled a sigh. He knew why they were there. His mother had made it a custom of hers to give useful gifts to the children of the marginalized community she had worked with for twenty-eight years. She had worked for an NGO that helped tribal women earn their livelihood by selling indigenous arts and also familiarizing them with horticulture and agroforestry.

"Nakul, get a pair of socks for yourself too. The weather is getting cold," she said while selecting socks and handkerchiefs.

"Don't want any," he said flatly.

Out of the corner of his eyes, he saw his mother glance at him briefly before going back to selecting the items.

At that moment, two people across the street caught his eyes. A middle-aged woman and a young woman of around his own age. Mother and daughter, he surmised. The young woman, grinning ear to ear, was checking stoles and scarves on display while her mother followed her, muttering something and making wild gestures with her hands.

The cacophony of their cackles and giggles shook and pierced Nakul's heart. His jaws tightened, and he looked away.

The younger woman had evoked a memory tucked within the deep grooves of his brain. His friends and their parents had come over to his house for some occasion. During play, one of his female friends fell and bruised her knee. Nakul's mother upbraided him, blaming him for chasing the girl and causing her fall. Though his female friend took it in her stride and seemed unfazed by her bruised knee, that wasn't the case with his mother. The dressing down he received that day remained etched into his head for days.

"What about these stoles, Nakul? Do you like any?"

His mother's voice pulled him to the present.

"I told you I don't want anything." Nakul didn't try to conceal his exasperation.

After dropping by a juice bar and a grocery store, they returned home. He went straight to his room. His mother had suggested they eat their lunch out, but Nakul had refused. He couldn't bear the idea of spending any more time with her than he already had.

......

Nakul had dozed off after his painting. He rubbed out the eye gunk from the corners of his eyes, and lifting his head, looked over at his painting of a fairy leaping through the air with her arms outstretched in front of her. It wasn't good, and it wasn't bad. Just like all his paintings. Yes, he was mediocre with colors, but that never discouraged him and made him quit. He hauled himself out of his bed and opened the bedroom door. The aroma of freshly brewed coffee hit him instantly. The aroma drew him to the kitchen. Empty kitchen. A tea pan was sitting on a burner, steam from it skittering towards the ceiling. He looked over his shoulder and turned back to the stove. He grabbed a cup from the cabinet and poured coffee in it. Carrying the cup, he walked out to the garden. The sky was preparing for its slumber. The pale gray light was slowly morphing into a darker shade. A warmth engulfed him as the hot coffee oozed down his throat. Nakul's eyes bounced from plant to plant and tree to tree.

He noticed a visitor on a solitary yellow hibiscus flower. A praying mantis was rocking from side to side in rhythmic motions. Then three things happened simultaneously: his mother's voice met his unprepared ears, the lamps in the garden lit up, and the praying mantis fell down from the flower.

"Oh, you're having your coffee."

Forcing a smile, Nakul turned sideways and lifted his half-empty cup as a gesture of acknowledgement.

"Nupur aunty was asking about you."

Nakul didn't say anything.

"Did you see the fishes in the pond?"

Nakul looked over to the backyard pond surrounded by rocks, pebbles, and plants. "I didn't know there were any fish in it."

"There are."

Nakul wanted to excuse himself and go to his room. But he didn't because he knew his mother wasn't finished talking to him.

"Want to share your plans for the future?"

Nakul groaned internally. "I told you I'll tell you soon. What is the hurry? Do you hate my presence so much?"

She took a step towards him. "Nakul, do you know what I hate the most? Indecisiveness. It was your decision to get a degree in design. It was your decision to study in Delhi. Then why is it so hard for you to decide what you want to do further? You're not a child anymore!"

"Was I ever a child to you?" Nakul retorted.

"Don't act like this, Nakul. All I'm asking you is to let me in on whatever decision you make."

"Right."

He found her gaze disquieting. He turned to the praying mantis, which had begun its torturously slow crawl back to the top of the plant.

"Being a parent is not easy. Especially being a single parent. But I did my duties, and I'm still doing everything that is required of me."

"Right."

After an excruciating minute, he heard footsteps retreating to the house. Nakul remained still, listening to the susurrating leaves rustling around him.

That night, he tried to recall the cause of the rift between him and his mother. It must have a beginning, right? But he couldn't pinpoint any particular cause. His mother had always kept him at arm's length. While growing up, he always felt alone at home.

Wasn't it the worst feeling? He'd often wonder. Feeling alone surrounded by people who were meant to love you.

The sense of being unmoored had always been with him at home. Except when…

In the dark, Nakul sat up and stretched his hand to press the light switch. Once the light flooded the room, Nakul looked at Oman with an affectionate smile. He remembered how attached he was to the doll. The doll would accompany him during quiet meals and while he did his homework. He'd press the doll to his chest and cry in his room, listening to his parents fight in the other room. The doll would whisper comfort to his ears in the dark. Nakul had forgotten all about it. He smiled at his younger self's imagination. Nakul covered the distance between them and took the doll out of the shelf. He then carried it with him to the bed and turned the light off.

......

Everything will be alright, Nakul. As long as I'm with you, I won't let anything hurt you. You sleep. Just sleep.

His eyes flew open. Sunlight streamed into his room through the window. He shifted to his other side and noticed Oman. Nakul told himself that the words he heard were part of a dream. Still, he struggled to recall any details of that dream, remembering only the comforting whispers of reassurance from someone. Slightly unsettled, Nakul shot out of bed and placed Oman back on the shelf.

After his morning ablution, he stepped out of his room. He immediately heard two voices, one familiar and one unfamiliar, coming from the dining room. He didn't understand why his mother couldn't seat the guest in the living room. He debated whether to go to the kitchen, past the dining room, in which case he'd have to face whoever was there with his mother, or stay within the safety of his room. Just then, his stomach growled, making the decision for him.

The women turned to him, pausing their conversation.

His mother smiled. "Nakul, do you remember Aksha aunty? She was our neighbor for many years. You know that pink house near the neem tree on our street? Her family used to live there. You used to play with her son, Pranit. Remember?"

Nakul managed a toothy grin and nodded. "Yes." He didn't. He didn't remember the woman or playing with her son, Pranit.

Both the women smiled, seemingly satisfied with his answer.

"Aksha came to invite us to her daughter's engagement on 14th," his mother said.

Nakul nodded again, his grin tapering to a smile.

"Nakul, you have to come with your mother, okay?" The woman said as she rose from her seat. "I should go now."

After five minutes, Nakul was in the kitchen, serving himself breakfast, when his mother walked towards him.

"Do you have anything to wear for the engagement, or should we go buy something for you?" She asked.

Quietly, Nakul carried his plate to the dining room. What he truly wished to do was take the plate to his room and eat there peacefully. But that wasn't allowed in his parents' house.

He sipped his coffee, ignoring his mother, who was looking at him and waiting for his response.

"I'm not going to the engagement," he said and braced himself.

His mother edged closer and grabbed hold of a chair's armrest. "What do you mean you're not going? Aksha invited us—you and me. You have to come with me."

"No, I'm not. Just because she invited me doesn't mean I have to go."

"Then why lie?" His mother's voice rose to a pitch.

Nakul forced his eyes on her. "What was I supposed to say then? Tell her the truth that I wasn't interested in attending her daughter's engagement or remember playing with her son?" he asked incredulously.

His mother mirrored his expression. "You lied about that as well?"

Frustration marred his face, and Nakul didn't try to conceal it. He shook his head, finding it pointless to carry on with the conversation.

"I'm not surprised; lying runs in your veins," his mother said, taking a dig at his father.

Frowning at his breakfast, Nakul asked, "Is this yesterday's?"

His mother's eyes flashed with indignation and anger. "You know I always prepare fresh meals, Nakul."

Nakul looked unconvinced. "Tastes spoiled to me. This chutney."

"Don't make things up, Nakul."

Shaking his head, Nakul stood up and strode to his room. He paused in the doorway, his eyes meeting his childhood companion, snugly sitting on the shelf, seemingly staring back at him. Beckoning him.

Everything will be alright, Nakul. As long as I'm with you, I won't let anything hurt you.

Nakul smiled. He entered his room and locked the door behind him.

13

SEED OF DOUBT

She opened the door and surveyed the baby blue and cream-coloured walls of the living room. She walked past it. Thistle purple walls covered one bedroom. Another room, navy blue. The kitchen and dining area were dusky saffron.

Nyla stepped onto the balcony of the navy blue room. Outside, neighbouring buildings and houses dominated the view. Nyla felt a prick of disappointment. She knew hoping for a stunning view from one's apartment balcony in a crowded city like Kolkata was an unrealistic expectation. With a sigh, she tilted her head back. A big, fluffy, white cloud momentarily blotted out the glare of the sun. Then, a cooing-like noise burst forth to her left, startling her. Startling her and causing her to turn towards the sound. Two doves were perched on the wooden cabinet mounted on the wall. Nyla let out a chuckle of relief, and her heart returned to its normal pace. One dove with head cocked to the side eyed Nyla suspiciously, while the other, unfazed, circled around, cooing.

"Well, hello. Nice spot you found there, huh? But you guys can't be here when I move in. You better find another house for yourself," Nyla said to the feathery creatures. Alarmed by her voice and her steady gaze on them, the birds flew away at once.

Nyla dug her phone out from her purse to call her boyfriend, Ari. She wanted to tell him she liked the apartment. Three weeks of house hunting finally came to an end. Since Ari was out of town on a conference, they'd decided that Nyla would check out the apartment by herself. Besides, he wasn't as picky as Nyla about finding the right home.

But the call went unanswered. Nyla fell completely still with her eyes locked onto her phone screen. When the screen went black, Nyla looked up. The sky had transformed into a vivid yellowish-orange, and Nyla instantly felt the warmth of the late morning sun on her skin. She turned and closed the door behind her.

Ten minutes later, she strolled down the street to familiarize herself with the place. Rows of tall trees with deep furrowed bark flanked the street. She was told that the residential colony was one of the oldest areas of Kolkata. Nyla's pace slowed, noting two old homes with weathered paint and green khorkhori windows. Picking up her speed, she noticed a ruckus occurring not far in front of her. Crows gathered on the overhead wires began cawing raucously. Oblivious to the noise were two middle-aged women with solemn expressions on their faces sitting on a stone bench outside a three-story house fringed with lush greenery. A little girl circled the bench, singing a rhyming song Nyla remembered from her childhood. Just then a vendor bicycled down the street, hawking his wares. Neither of the women looked up. A little further, a magpie robin was singing, perched on the lower branches of an Indian almond tree. Nyla tilted her face to the dappled sunlight peeking at her through the foliage of trees. She wished Ari was there with her.

She stopped dead in her tracks when she saw it. It was a public cemetery, appearing neglected with wild shrubs reclaiming the gravesites. She hesitated briefly before moving towards it. She sauntered through the crumbling tombstones, reading the name, date of birth, and date of death of some of the long dead. The occupants of three tombs were nearly 300 years old. She tried not to imagine the stories of each one. Nyla paused in front of a seemingly new tomb. There was a carved photograph of a woman on the headstone. Nyla leaned over. The dead was a young woman. Just like her. Nyla straightened and turned. She noticed something in her periphery and almost shrieked seeing what looked like an elbow from behind a tree. A lone, giant, knobbly tree amidst the dead. Ignoring her pounding heart, Nyla advanced towards the tree. Before she could see the owner of the hand, she saw a woman with long silver hair crouched next to a headstone. Nyla inched further and came upon a middle-aged man sitting at the base of the tree, his back against the aged tree trunk. He looked up at her with an impassive face.

Before Nyla could think, the man turned to the silver-haired woman and said coolly, "My wife."

Nyla looked back and forth at the couple. She didn't know what to say.

"And that's my son's grave," the man said. Again, Nyla wasn't sure what to say, or to say anything at all.

With her eyes fixed on the headstone, the woman rocked back and forth. As Nyla watched with unease, the woman suddenly stilled and looked across at them. A grin cracked her solemn face, and she waved at them. The scene looked odd to Nyla.

A gust of wind blew, lifting the dry leaves off the ground.

“She wears the same clothes every time we come here. It was a gift from him. My son.”

The man’s voice jolted Nyla. For a brief moment, she had forgotten about him. She noticed his wrinkly hands with protruding veins resting on his knees trembled slightly. His unwavering gaze remained fixed on his wife.

Nyla looked at the woman, dressed in a white kurti and turquoise pants. The woman leaned over the headstone, mouthing something.

“If left on her own, she’d spend hours here, perhaps even spend the night. She likes talking to him. Unlike me, she doesn’t mind not getting any response.”

“How?” Nyla didn’t realize she voiced her thoughts aloud.

The man looked at her. “Hit and run. It’s been four years now. Some days, I wake up in an empty house. I’d come here directly. I’d just know she’d be here.”

A deep resonant sound of metal being struck rang repeatedly at a distance.

An unreasonable sense of being watched nudged her. Nyla whirled around and found no one.

"It's quite natural to feel that way. As if someone's watching you," the man said, looking back at his wife.

Her stomach clenched. Instinctively, Nyla took a step back. Did the man just read her mind?

"Many do. Though I never did," the man explained without turning to her.

Unsettled by the man's ability to sense her unease without even looking at her, Nyla stared at him, dumbfounded. A sad smile erupted on his face, and he looked down, shaking his head. Nyla looked over to his wife fervently brushing the dust off the stone slab covering the grave. It didn't escape Nyla's notice that it was the only granite tombstone in the cemetery. Feeling somber, Nyla gazed down at her feet, where a black garden ant was battling with the sturdy weeds inches from her.

"Are you married?" the man asked.

Her head snapped up. The question took Nyla by surprise. Why would he want to know her marital status? The man was looking at her as a weary teacher might regard a distracted student.

"No," Nyla responded.

The man shifted his eyes to a gravestone to her side. "It is better that way. No one will break your heart."

Her response was immediate: "I have a boyfriend though. We live together."

The man didn't say anything.

With silence invading their space, Nyla wondered if she should leave. Her eyes fell to her feet again, and she reminded herself to cut her overgrown toenails when she returned home.

"He wasn't a happy man. My son. His girlfriend was like a thorn to his happiness. He loved her dearly. But she wasn't faithful to him. He was working for a tech company in Bangalore when he met her. He wanted to marry her. We were ready. A year into their relationship, his girlfriend moved back to her family home here. She said she wanted to stay in Kolkata. As per her wish, he quit his job in Bangalore and moved back as well. He got a job soon after and was eager to settle down with her. But gradually we noticed changes in him. He seemed worried all the time. He never shared anything with us. But we, as parents, knew something wasn't going well in his relationship. His girlfriend kept postponing the date of their engagement. She kept making excuses."

Something crawled on her big right toe. Nyla lifted her foot and shook it. The black ant, back on the ground, moved on unperturbed.

"Never trust them."

"Excuse me?" Nyla wasn't sure if she had missed something.

The man looked at her again. His puffy, drooping eyelids seemed as if they'd fall over his world-weary eyes at any moment.

"Trust nobody!" He hissed. "Trust nobody, as they'll just give you pain and nothing else. They hide. They lie. They cheat. They bruise you. And they're never honest with you."

"That's not true," Nyla opined. She was ready to leave. She took a step back to signal that she was leaving.

The man smiled wryly. "Really? How much do you know about your boyfriend?"

The question irked her. "Everything." But as soon as the word tumbled out of her mouth, a small voice in her mind needled. Did she really know everything about Ari?

The man shook his head, looking amused. His reaction grated on her.

Her brain ordered her to leave, but her feet didn't move. Nyla didn't know why. She turned her gaze on the man's wife and found the woman's eyes fixed on her. Uneasiness washed over her, and Nyla looked away.

"Oh, she thinks she knows her partner through and through." The man mouthed, staring vacantly ahead.

There. There it was. The pesky seed of doubt. Nyla had vowed she'd never allow the seed of doubt to ruin her relationship the way it had broken her parents' marriage. The malicious seed of doubt her paternal aunts had sown into the mind of her gullible father, resulting in her parents' constant fights and eventual divorce, would never enter her life. She had steered clear of it. But, to her dismay, something shifted within her. She could feel it. Yes, she could. Like indefatigable rainwater seeping through waterproof walls, the germ of doubt was attempting to penetrate her vulnerable mind.

"Does he make you happy?" The man didn't look at her. He was smiling at his wife the way an affectionate parent would at a child.

Of course Ari made her happy. They might not be a married couple, but they were just like one. Nyla wanted to say it out loud, but the words jammed in her throat.

"Y-yes," Nyla stammered.

Yes, he made her happy. Didn't he? Yes, he had some traits that irked her, but wasn't that normal with everyone? Yes, there were days when she wished he'd talk to her about his feelings. But wasn't it his cool demeanor that drew her to him? Yes! Then why complain? She'd heard that qualities that attract at first often become irksome later.

"Interesting. Is there absolutely nothing you dislike about him?" The man's voice lowered a pitch. His face took on a serene look. And his eyes were closed.

"No," lied Nyla immediately.

Yes, she hated when Ari would ignore some of her questions and, upon repeating them, would look at her as if her questions were frivolous and not worth answering.

Yes, she hated when his demeanor would instantly change in the presence of his friends. He'd become a stranger to her.

Yes, she hated when he sometimes avoided answering where he was.

"Love is very alluring, isn't it? It draws us in and bewitches us. And when we begin to lose our individuality because of it, it lifts up its veil and shows us its true color. Love is an affliction. Look where my son's love ended him," said the man, his voice full of anguish and contempt.

Nyla wanted to remind him that his son's girlfriend, whether faithful or not, was not responsible for his accident. But she kept quiet. Instead, she mulled over the man's bleak outlook on love.

Love is an affliction? She didn't wish to see love that way. But she also wasn't unaware of the pernicious side of love.

The man's wife rose, smoothing her pants.

"Ready to go home?" The man called out. The woman shook her head, her gray hair glistening in the sunlight.

"I used to love her hair. Her hair used to be longer than this, falling below the waist. My son wasn't a fan of long hair. He thought it made her look old-fashioned. So he made her cut it."

A memory escaped from the shadows and danced before her mind's eyes.

The glistening scattered shards of glass on the cream floor tiles. She looked at them, betraying no emotions. Nyla crouched to collect the pieces of glass. Ari joined her. She lifted her eyes to him. But Ari didn't meet her eyes. He stood abruptly.

"Don't you trust me?" He asked, looking mildly flustered.

With the broken glass pieces in her cupped hands, Nyla rose with confusion and mild annoyance. "Did I say that?

Ari looked agitated, confusing Nyla further. "Then don't ask me about whoever calls me."

Nyla's heart sank. "What is wrong with that? I just asked you who the girl was who kept calling you since morning."

"She's a friend of mine."

"You could have simply said that."

"She's moving houses and needs some help with that."

"I didn't ask for an explanation, Ari." Nyla had walked past him to the kitchen.

So lost she was in her reverie that she didn't notice the man hauling himself to a standing position and striding towards his wife.

Nyla was back to the present. She watched as the man moved closer to his wife, who began shaking her head vigorously. It didn't take long before the man trudged back, holding the hand of his reluctant wife with mournful eyes.

As they walked past her, the man gave her a nod and a small smile.

Once alone, Nyla looked around her surroundings. The dead were quiet. She moved towards the gravestone of the man's son. The seed of doubt had already sent out a little root into the fertile ground of her mind. Something was growing from it rapidly. A plant of...

Her phone rang. Nyla knew who it was from the ringtone before she dug it out from her purse. She answered it.

"Hey, I'm leaving in the evening. The train is at 5. Be there by 10 in the morning," Ari's voice came from the other side.

Nyla didn't say anything. She was just as quiet as the dead around her.

"Hello? Ny?"

"Yeah, yeah, I'm here. I heard you."

"I'll arrive in the morning."

"Oh, okay."

No sound reached her from the other side for a few seconds.

"Wow, that was...that was a lukewarm response. Are you alright? Did you go check the apartment? Did you like it?" Ari said.

A heavy weariness settled upon her. "Yeah, I did. The apartment is just fine."

"Oh. So, do you want to keep looking, or will this 'just fine' apartment do for us?"

"Let's talk about it tomorrow, okay." Nyla ended the call without hearing Ari's response.

She retraced her steps and walked out of the eerie silence of the departed ones.

~The End~